Damien Dsoul was born in Port Harcourt, Nigeria. He has written numerous contemporary novels in different genres, such as *Mary's Addiction*, *The Story of Caya*, and *Father's Land*, to name a few. He has also published collections of short stories and screenplays. He is quite active online, and when he isn't writing, he dabbles in amateur photography and collects old coins.

To Steve Olesky, a true friend.

Damien Dsoul

A Horny Gilf Named Erica

AUSTIN MACAULEY PUBLISHERS®
LONDON • CAMBRIDGE • NEW YORK • SHARJAH

Ordering Information
Quantity sales: Special discounts are available on quantity purchases by corporations, associations, and others. For details, contact the publisher at the address below.

Publisher's Cataloging-in-Publication data
Dsoul, Damien
A Horny Gilf Named Erica

ISBN 9798891559318 (Paperback)
ISBN 9798891559325 (ePub e-book)

Library of Congress Control Number: 2024918652

www.austinmacauley.com/us

First Published 2024
Austin Macauley Publishers LLC
40 Wall Street, 33rd Floor, Suite 3302
New York, NY 10005
USA

mail-usa@austinmacauley.com
+1 (646) 5125767

Table of Contents

1

Babysitting a Gilf

My boyfriend, Terrance, was fucking me one hot summer afternoon when he suddenly called me a Gilf. Until that day, I'd never been privy to that word or knew what it meant. I was swept up in my explicit emotions, reeling with unbridled lust while he attacked me from behind. He lifted my face off the bed, turned me sideways so he could kiss my lips, then whispered that I was his 'Gilf whore!' It wasn't until later while recuperating from our concluded sex that I inquired what that word meant.

"What, you ain't heard that word before?" He looked surprised when I asked him.

"No, I haven't," I chuckled while I caressed his hairy chest. "You know me, babe. I don't keep up with whatever the young ones out there are into."

"You don't have to be young to figure out that word, babe. You've heard of the word 'Milf', right?"

"Yeah. Mothers I'd love to fuck; everybody knows that one."

"Gilf is the version for mature wives: Grannies I'd love to fuck. Get it?"

"Oh, wow. I never thought of that. You're such a nasty devil, thinking that's all I am to you."

"That ain't all of what you are to me, babe," Terrance lifted a pair of my tits to his face. "You're just so damn sexy," he cooed. "I won't mind fucking you on a daily basis."

"Hmmm, you know I'd love nothing more than that, darling," I purred.

I rolled onto him, kissing him while teasing my pussy against his cock that was growing hard again. His hands caressed my butt before sliding underneath to tickle my pussy with his erection. I wanted his cock in the best way. I wrenched his turgid member off his grip and drove it into my cunt. I exhaled as I felt that familiar warmth explode inside me. Goosebumps popped across my arm. I could feel the tiny hairs on the back of my neck stand upright as my pussy swallowed his cock.

"Ohhhhh fuck!" I gasped while grinding my butt against his crotch. I leaned forward and kissed him. "I love your cock so fucking much," I moaned.

"Hmmm, too bad you can't take it home with you."

I crackled at his humor, knowing it was true. "I know, babe. Fuck me one last time for the road," I exhaled with passion. "Fuck me harder this time."

Terrence knew what I wanted when it came to sex and was never lacking when it came time to give it to me. He never balked or hesitated to fuck me like a whore, like I almost didn't matter to him. Sex with him was always intense and rowdily enjoyable, like riding the world's scariest rollercoaster. He took charge of me immediately and began jerking his hips, slamming his cock into my vagina aggressively. He smacked my butt repeatedly, making me groan frantically. I kept grinding my butt against his crotch, squealing wild and raunchy while his cock stretched my cunt. I kept mouthing off, telling him how much I loved getting fucked by him, how much I looked forward each week to enjoying him; I would have killed if a week passed and I never got to have wild fun with him.

He fucked me to my utter satisfaction. He made me cream over his cock as my body quivered from impending climax.

An hour later, I wore my clothes and kissed him goodbye before leaving his apartment. I wore my shades as I left his building, stepped out into the evening sun, got into my car, and drove home. My husband, Richard, hadn't missed me the entire afternoon that I was gone. He had entertained several of his friends who'd come over to watch a game while I'd lied that I'd gone swimming at the YMCA establishment located in the city.

Gilf.

The word reoccurred in my mind later that night as I lay beside my snoring husband. Who would have thought that I'd reached Gilf status? I was baffled whether to take it as a compliment or an insult to be labeled as one. Where did my middle-age period go? I was approaching my mid-fifties, having given birth to three kids and being rewarded, so far, with five grandkids. Yet, I didn't feel old or rusty; neither Richard nor I felt ready for the nursing home. Richard was semi-retired from practicing law. I work part-time as a paralegal for a federal NGO outfit. It sounds boring, but it keeps me busy and ensures me enough excuses to drive to the city and spend lots of quality time with Terrance.

Richard knows nothing about Terrance, and that's the way I want it to remain. I always looked forward to seeing him again. The thought of feeling him naked against me always got my blood pumping. I knew he had younger women he dated on the side, and I didn't care; whenever I'm with him, it's all about us and nobody else. When I'm with him, the last thing that occurs to me is our age difference.

Days later, Terrance gave me a surprise call to let me know he was close to my home. A week had passed since the last time we fooled around. I would have gone to him, except I was babysitting one of my grandkids and had no excuses to give. This was one necessary setback to being a Grannie.

As it turns out, Richard was away at work when Terrance showed up at our doorstep. I was alarmed to see him, even though I welcomed him inside while carrying my one-year-old grandson, Jeff, in my arms.

"Terrance, you shouldn't be here," I told him. "Richard might be home any minute."

"He ain't gonna be home till four, babe, and you know it," he said. "I missed you and figured I'd come to you instead," he kissed me. "You on grandmotherly duty?"

"Yeah. My daughter's off with her husband to visit her in-laws, so I'm babysitting until tonight. I was going to give you a call later."

"No point in waiting later, babe," he smiled broadly. "I'll be your babysitter, and I'm here to take good care of you. But first, how about we put your little man to bed and then get comfy."

I couldn't believe Terrance had the audacious nerve to come to my home while I was supposed to babysit my grandkid. We've had sex in my home before, but this was different…and sort of kinky, too. He was such an incorrigible fellow who hardly took no for an answer, which was a quality I liked about him.

"Come with me," I said, leading him upstairs to my bedroom.

I went and gently placed my grandson in his crib beside my bed. He was asleep, so I knew he wouldn't be too much trouble to watch. I turned and locked arms around Terrance and kissed him, feeling suddenly hungry for him.

"I wasn't looking forward to you coming over," I cooed. "But since you're here…"

"Let's make good use of our time," he concluded.

He relieved me of my clothes, and I did likewise to him. I lay on the bed and lifted my legs while Terrance played with my breasts before sliding his face down my abdomen. I closed my eyes briefly and squirmed as his tongue made contact with my pussy. His tongue performed sexual surgery on me, the way he lolled, probed, and sucked my pussy's nectar. My breathing grew laborious, and my body jerked and squirmed spasmodically the longer he ate my cunt.

"Awww…Awwhhh, Terrance," I moaned amid gasps. "Ohh, babe, don't fucking stop."

I glanced at the crib periodically to ensure my grandson, Jeff, was snugly asleep. So far, so good.

Terrance came on top, and I tasted my cunt's juice off his lips. His prick slid against my vulva, arousing me further. I grabbed his cock and inserted it into my vagina. I bit my lower lip as he thrust deep inside me.

The pain was exquisite.

I couldn't hold my moan as he buried more inches inside me.

I hugged him tight, wanting more of what he had to give.

Terrance worked his hips and offered me more exquisite thrusts of his cock. I laid on my back, fighting the sexual tide that seemed keen on drowning me. I wanted to let loose—become my wild self—to buck and squeal my loudest but had to hold myself out of fear of waking my grandkid. Terrance sensed this and did his best to keep in line with me. He fucked me slow but steady. I raked my nails across his backside and sometimes dared him to quicken his pace like he often did. I almost didn't care about waking up Seth or fearing that Richard might be heading home that minute.

I wanted to be sexually fulfilled.

"Fill me up, babe," I muttered. "Give me everything you've got."

Terrance pulled out and propped me to get on my elbows and knees. He hunched over my backside and rammed his cock into my pussy. I grabbed the sheets and cried into the pillow's fabric as he fucked me harder and harder. Our bodies made smacking noises, and I kept checking to make sure the baby wasn't stirring in his crib. My moans grew louder as I felt an orgasm stirring inside my womb. The excitement was too much for me to bear.

I squeezed my eyes shut and bit down on the sheets as I felt an orgasm roar inside my gut.

Terrance continued fucking me as if nothing had happened. A shiver ran through my body as I suffered the onslaught of my sudden climax. Terrance gripped my waist and tore into me harder until an intense moment arrived, and he ejaculated inside me. I waited until he had concluded his business before falling flat on my face.

My grandson did stir awake, but that was after we had cleaned ourselves up and I changed the sheets. I opened the windows and sprayed some potpourri fragrance to consume the stench of sex in the room; I lit some incense, too. I carried Seth with me as I escorted Terrance out of the house. I kissed him and said he would text me later, and then I waved goodbye before returning inside. My daughter and her son returned later that evening to pick up their son. Nobody found out about my afternoon romp, and that's still my secret adventure.

2

Foreplay at the YMCA with a Gilf

I riffled through my bedside cabinet, looking for my bathing lotion. It took seconds before I remembered where I had previously left it inside my other handbag, and I immediately got it and threw it into my gym bag. I was hurrying to leave the house to head out to the YMCA, where I often enjoyed swimming weekly.

It was a Saturday and I was lucky I wouldn't be babysitting any of my grandkids today. But who knew how long that freedom would last? Any moment now, my phone might ring and it would be one of my kids demanding if I was free to look after their little ones because they had some scheduled date to enjoy, and it was too late to find anyone else to take the task. Trust me, I've gotten that aggravating request plenty of times before. Today, I was determined not to be held back, not even by my husband, Richard. *Good heavens, especially not him!*

I rechecked the contents of my bag to ensure I had everything I needed before grabbing my cell phone. I looked at myself in the mirror—not bad-looking for a gregarious old broad—gave myself the OK sign and exited the room. Richard was downstairs watching a golf tournament game like he couldn't think of anything less boring to enjoy. I told him I was off to the YMCA. He waved at me and told me to have a good time. I snorted derisively. It wasn't like I expected him to get off the couch and walk me out to the car as I opened the door.

I wore my shades as I stepped outside, got into my car, started the engine, and then was off to the YMCA.

It was a gorgeous Saturday afternoon. I basked in the feel of the wind ruffling my hair as I drove, observing the easy-going traffic while mouthing off to the country-rock music blasting off my stereo. My phone lay on the passenger seat, looking neglected. It occurred to me that it might suddenly start ringing and it would be one of my kids making an emergency call. I was tempted to switch it off, but what if I missed a crucial call? No, let it be for now.

I drove to Marlborough County, a seven-mile drive from my home, where the YMCA building was located. There were others close by, but it was for a particular reason that I signed up there.

The YMCA parking lot was usually filled with dozens of cars, but to my surprise, it was empty when I arrived. I turned off my engine and grabbed my gym bag and cell phone before getting out. I looked around to make sure I wasn't being delusional; the parking lot was devoid of any vehicle besides mine. I keyed in my vehicle alarm before walking to the building.

I made straight for the changing room, which was empty like I didn't think it would be. The day was starting to feel eerie, but it wasn't unusual. I had been the first visitor at the

YMCA a few times, but that was years ago, back when I first started, and it wasn't to this one. This was probably the first time I arrived here and found myself alone. I went into the Ladies' Room and changed into my bathing suit. I figured it wouldn't be long before others started arriving. I might as well enjoy having the place to myself.

I wrapped my towel around my neck, folded my clothes into my gym bag, and then left to go and take a dip in the pool.

The swimming pool area was empty; the water looked inviting. I dipped my feet into the shallow edge and watched the water ripple. I turned my head when I heard a door close somewhere. I looked around and waited, but nobody appeared—there was nobody except me.

I strolled toward the pool's deep end and lowered myself to sit on the edge while dipping and kicking my feet in the water, creating splashes and waves. The water felt pleasing enough to pop goosebumps on my arms. I leaned backward and shut my eyes, smiling languorously while still creating havoc with the pool water; my cell phone lay beside me, undisturbed.

My eyes stayed shut, but my ears caught footsteps approaching my direction. I didn't panic even when the person's shadow loomed over me or when he laid his hands on my shoulders, caressing my skin like he intended to give me a soothing massage. I smiled as I inhaled the musk-like fragrance that always pervaded him whenever I was in his presence.

"You've been waiting here long?" Terence, my secret lover, asked.

He was the reason I signed up with this particular YMCA club since he lived nearby. It was an excellent way to be close to him without arousing suspicion from Richard or my kids, who had no idea their mom was a black cock-whore!

"Hmmm, not long enough," I said, reaching for his arm as his hands were busily running down my swimsuit, making my nipples hard behind the fabric. I opened my eyes to stare at him. "I thought you weren't going to show up; I didn't see your car in the parking lot."

"That's because I just got here," he said. "You beat me to the punch."

"Hmmm, I guess you're going to have to then pay the price for being late. Though I don't know how long we'll have this place to ourselves."

"Then let's not wait any longer. Stay here, don't move an inch."

Terence jumped into the water and broke to the surface seconds later. He swam toward me with his face inches from my crotch.

"Mind pulling that to the side?" He indicated my swimsuit. "I need to see what I'm working with."

Usually, I wouldn't dare attempt this—Terence is fond of making bold, audacious acts that I consider too outrageous and exciting—but I was committed already, so I allowed him to do whatever, knowing it would get me off, too. I looked about to establish that we were alone in the pool area before sliding my panties to expose my pussy to him. Terence drew closer and parted my thighs so he could breathe upon my cunt. I gasped and rolled my eyes when his tongue tasted my pussy.

"Wow! Oh my God, Terrence, *you're insane!*"

I was frightened and exhilarated by what he was doing. I worried that the glass doors would burst open and people would suddenly pour into the pool area any minute, but simultaneously, this was way too audacious, and I didn't want him to stop. Terrence didn't seem to want to stop what he was doing either. His body kept floating under the water while his face stayed above the surface as he worked his tongue into my pussy. I couldn't hold back the orgasmic tremor erupting inside me. My body trembled so badly that I couldn't control myself from slapping my palm against my thighs.

"Stop, Terrence," I gasped. "Please…please, darling, stop…I beg you. Let's go…let's go someplace far better than here."

Terrence listened to me, and thankfully, he agreed.

He pulled himself out of the pool and came and helped me to my feet. My phone suddenly began to ring. The call was from my daughter. I switched off my phone, linked my arm around Terrence, and then headed to our separate changing rooms.

Terrence was waiting for me when I came out—we were back in our clothes. People were then entering the pool area. I exchanged greetings with several women while Terence walked ahead of me. I wasn't too friendly with any women at the club; neither knew about our relationship.

Outside, Terence signaled me over to his car; we always drove in his car to arouse less suspicion in case anyone thought I was away. I got into the passenger seat, and he unzipped his jeans. My head stayed on his crotch with his cock jammed in my mouth while he drove to his place. His cock stayed hard in my mouth, and I even attempted to wiggle my hand further into his jeans to play with his balls; he usually loves it when I do that. We arrived there minutes later, and he parked his car, and then we went inside.

We didn't make it to the bedroom, not right away.

3

Sex and No Lunch with a Gilf

Terrence opened his apartment door and shoved me inside. He slammed the door shut, and then we discarded our bags, including other essentials, before attacking each other like hungry lions. I wanted him so bad, as he equally desired me.

We clashed and started kissing in a frenzy. My arms locked around his shoulders, my fingers dug into the fabric of his shirt while he squeezed and caressed me tight like he worried I might turn into vapor and disappear. Our lips smacked as our tongues roamed each other's mouths while we exchanged fluids. My eyes were half-shut, but I could see him clear as day as I could feel his hands grabbing my butt, fighting to dig into my clothes. My body was still wet from having showered in the YMCA changing room. His clothes, too, were wet; he had probably dried himself in a rush to meet me outside the changing room before we left the club.

Terrence led me into his living room; it was his kingdom, and I was a visiting emissary. Terrence was single and was in high demand for other women. There have been times when we spoke on the phone and I heard some other women's voice in the background, interrupting our talk, but

I never fretted. I knew the game—I was nearly twenty years older than him. By all accounts, we shouldn't even be dating, but here we are, and I'm grateful for whatever time I enjoyed his company, especially knowing it would lead to sex.

We were hurrying out of our clothes when we fell clumsily on his sofa. I nearly ripped off my buttons while he scrambled to get me out of my clothes. His fly was unzipped, and his cock dangled out in turgid majesty. I grabbed it, pulled it to my face, and hungrily sucked him while he squeezed and caressed my breasts.

I made room for Terrence to settle beside me, then came and knelt before him to suck his cock better. I slid my hand between my thighs, fingering my eager cunt, moaning in my mouth as I continued to pleasure his cock. Hard to believe an old fart like me would be making out like a whore before a young man like Terrence. Even hard to imagine that he had no qualms fucking me with the type of vicious he would give to someone of his age range.

"That's enough of that, slut," he informed me. "Come sit on this black dick."

I swiped saliva off my lips before rising to my feet and coming to straddle him.

My massive, stretch-marked butt cheeks settled on his thighs while simultaneously his cock impaled me up to my chest. I grabbed the sofa's headrest and cried as it felt like I could feel his cock pressed against the walls of my throat. Fucking Terrence always felt like the first time, regardless of how long we've been seeing each other. His cock was too incredible—unforgettable—I feel I'd lose my mind if I never got to enjoy him again.

I waited for my pussy to get acquainted with him inside me before daring myself to start jerking my muscles. My hips felt suddenly stiff like they couldn't remember the mechanics that usually comes with sex. It took some seconds before my body responded better and another while before the exhilaration got me whipped, drawing me closer to a climax. My large breasts jiggled and brushed against his face; Terrence got compelled to suck each pair, further heightening my arousal.

"Oh God, you're so fucking amazing!" I gasped.

Terrence caressed my backside, smacked my rump, and then pulled my face down for a kiss. My hips were jerking harder now; I could feel my buttocks clench each time I grind against his pelvis. The feel of his cock got me exhaling harder; it felt like I was swimming the deep end of the pool while fighting to breathe. This was how I often felt whenever Terrence stuck his cock inside me—he always knew how to knock my breath away.

I lifted myself, planted my feet on his sofa while gripping his shoulders, and continued lowering myself down his shaft. Terrence wedged the underside of my butt with his hands and started working his hips and thighs. His thighs slapped against my butt while I groaned from the contact of him thrusting his cock up and down my cunt. At some point he held me tight, grunting heavily as he lifted me off the sofa. He rolled his arms under my thighs, lifted me higher, and resumed jerking his hips, slapping his pelvis against my crotch. Terrence struggled to hold me while I began working my pelvis at him, jerking my thighs up and against his arms, wanting more of his cock inside me. I didn't want the feeling to end, at least not yet.

Terrence carted me off into a corridor that led to his bedroom. He kicked open the door and threw me halfway across to land on his bed. I lay on my back with my legs spread and my pussy winking at him.

"You'd better come and get it while it's still hot," I laughed.

His cock was the most beautiful sword I'd ever beheld as he held my legs apart before sliding into me. I grabbed his butt, and it was then my turn to smack his ass cheeks while he hammered me deep. He slid his arms under my backside; my legs stayed as further apart as I could make them, grunting and gasping while he fucked me harder and harder.

"Whose pussy is this?" He grunted.

"It's your pussy," I gasped. "It's your pussy, babe!"

"I can't hear you. Whose pussy?"

"Your pussy!" I hollered. "Awwhh, it's your fucking pussy!"

His pace increased. Terrence was breathing against my face, holding my legs apart while ramming me with all his might. My screams filled the room—it excited and scared me to hear my screams. His body kept slamming into me, forcing me to see stars.

I didn't merely see stars; I saw a constellation of galaxies.

At some point, I heard myself choking on my cries like they struck a well in my throat. I tried glancing beyond my abdomen at the sight of his cock pounding my pussy. My eyes were watery with tears. I was pleading in my head for Terrence to hurry along with his climax. I couldn't take the suspense anymore.

Terrence's cock was like a nuclear bomb ready to explode inside me—I felt it growing hot each second. He tensed, wrapped his arms around my thighs, and nearly lifted me off the bed. Our sweaty bodies collided as I then heard him roar like a lion announcing his presence.

His cock had swelled twice its size—its moment had finally arrived.

I shut my eyes, tightened my grip around his arms, and yelled at him to cum inside me, "Give me everything, babe! I want everything!"

He did. Spurt after spurt of semen flooded my pussy; I had never been so relieved when he lowered me back to his bed.

Terrence lit a cigarette and then lay beside me. He placed an ashtray on his chest and blew smoke into the air. The odor in the room was a mixture of cigarettes, semen, cum juice, and sweat—the perfect mixture of a salacious afternoon fuck-fest. It was way past an hour since we left the YMCA. My phone had stayed switched off since. I had no idea if my daughter had attempted to call me since, and I didn't care. I should have been home already to make lunch for Richard, but I didn't care about that either. This was where I wanted to be, this moment especially.

"I wish this moment didn't have to end," I murmured while I cuddled beside him.

"What else would you prefer?"

"You and me here in bed, without a care of whatever's out there. I won't need to return home except stay here with you."

"Someone's gonna be looking for you," Terrence remarked. "Either your man or one of your kids. They're gonna find me, and it ain't gonna be good."

"I could leave him," I bit my lip when I uttered those words. I shouldn't have said it, but this was a usual feeling that absorbed me whenever Terrence and I got done fucking. I start thinking sporadic thoughts, like how great it would be to leave my husband, kids, and grandkids behind and come to be with him.

"You shouldn't be thinking that," he said. "My dick's got you thinking crazy."

"I'm too old for you, I know. You deserve someone better and younger, like your other women."

"Ain't no younger women here except you. How about we stay focused on what we've got and leave out other nonsense stuff."

"Every time I finish having sex with you, for some reason, I feel like it's going to be our last. I don't know why I keep thinking that."

"Yeah, I wonder," he blew a cloud of smoke into the air.

I rested my head on my arm to observe him better. "Do you ever think the same whenever we finish fucking, or is it just me?"

"I do sometimes, yeah."

"Come on, be honest. You're only saying that to make me happy."

"I'm being honest." He extinguished his cigarette, then returned the ashtray to his bedside table before turning to me. "This is me being serious, babe. You are an incredibly sexy woman for your age. Matters not how old you are, but ain't no woman I've met that's as special as you. What you and I have here is special for us; let's not try to jinx it by thinking crazy."

"I don't know…I want to believe you, but I feel one of these days, I won't hear from you again. Like you're going to think of me as too old or something."

"Come here."

He took my arm and had me straddle him. His penis was asleep, but it took a little wiggling effort on my part before it started nudging itself to life. I knew what Terrence wanted as he, too, knew what I wanted.

I lifted myself, inserted his cock into my vagina, and began to ride him like before.

4

When a Gilf Gets Caught!

It had been a long and tiresome day for me. I left Terrence's place as reluctant as usual, returned to get my car at the YMCA, and stopped by a Whole Foods supermarket not far from home to purchase some items before driving home. My daughter, Linda, had dropped by, and she and her kids were home awaiting my belated arrival. It was a good thing I had stayed away, or else I'd have been stuck with babysitting duty as usual; today was one of those days I considered myself fortunate, though I got to spend some pleasurable time with my grandkids before they left. Richard hadn't missed me much, though he was sour because his favorite team had lost the game he had previously watched. Tough luck.

The rest of the day went like clockwork: I made dinner and we later chatted about everything else while watching a Netflix movie. I had almost blocked Terrence off my mind until I showered that night and recalled sublime moments spent with him. Even he had been disinclined to me leaving, which was surprising. It let me know how much he desired me.

Later that evening, Richard and I lay in bed, about to retire. Usually, that's when I like to catch up on some reading, anything to make my eyes weary for the oncoming sleep. Richard was perusing some news on his tablet while listening to jazz music on his earphones. We were lost to our individual world when he eventually placed his tablet on his bedside cabinet, took off his reading glasses and earphones, then turned toward me.

"So, Erica, when are you going to tell me about him?"

I turned to him, baffled. "What?"

He didn't say anything but stare at me. There was more to his stare. It drove a wedge of fear up my spine and gave me a foreboding look at what was coming that I was ill-prepared for.

"What are you talking about, Rich?"

"I'm talking about the black guy you've been fucking for several weeks now," he said. "You know who I'm talking about, Erica. Let's not play games."

My heart skipped an instant beat. This must be a dream, I thought. No way could this possibly be real.

"Terrance," Richard said. "That's his name, right? Terrance. You want me to tell you where he lives, too? Maybe that would help jog your memory a bit."

I closed my book and let my feet fall flat on the bed while he patiently awaited my response. My immediate thought was to craft some quick lie—anything to stall for time—but the look in Richard's eyes told me that was futile. He would know I was lying, and that would make things worse.

"How long have you known?" I asked.

"I've known for a while now," he said. "You weren't always as smart as you thought you were, Erica. We went to see him today, right?"

"I went swimming," I retorted. "At the YMCA, like I told you I was going."

"Right. And then you left with your lover-boy to his place."

"That's the way it ended, yes."

"It wouldn't be the first time." Richard looked away momentarily before speaking, "We've been through this before, Erica. You promised you weren't going to do anything stupid behind my back again."

"You promised to take good care of my needs, Richard. You said you would be there for me sexually. Where did that promise go?"

"You know about my debilitating problem, Erica. Don't play dumb like you aren't aware. I'm not the man I used to be ten or five years ago, but that doesn't give you any right to play around without telling me about it."

I swung my feet off the bed and paced the room, using what little time I had to gather my strength before facing him.

"Let's say I'd told you about Terrence before he and I started, Richard. Would you have agreed to us meeting for just sex and nothing else?"

It was a reach, I know, but I had no other option.

"I would have given it some good thought," he replied.

"It's funny, but anytime you use those words, it means no. Tell the truth, Rich. You never would have agreed to me having someone on the side. You would have been apoplectic with rage if you knew."

"I should be apoplectic right now, but I'm not," he said with a tight voice. "Don't try deflecting from the issue here, Erica. You're the one who's messed up by cheating on me, and you've no idea how upset I am about that. How would you feel if I'd told our daughter about your infidelity? What sort of mother would that make you?"

I stopped in my tracks. Yes, I suddenly realized the truth—I had messed up. I had been selfish not to have told him, but for adequate reasons, knowing he would have forced me to end my relationship with Terrence. It wasn't our first time involved in such a dilemma. Once, there had been a time when Richard had no problem sharing me with other men. But then, he'd begun having kidney issues that grew terrible over time. It cut our swinging lifestyle abruptly short. Where I had wanted to continue, feeling sexually neglected for years, Richard decided he was out of the game, and thus I, too, had no choice but to discontinue.

But that was until I encountered Terrence. He had renewed my sexual curiosity in ways I had never thought before. Overnight, I had gone from being a sex-starved mature wife to a horny Gilf.

"Why was it Terrence, Erica?" Richard asked. "I'm curious to know whatever attracted him to you."

"Wouldn't you like to know, Rich? He made me feel…special. Special in ways I hadn't felt before. How long has it been since you and I last had fun together?"

"Years," Richard admitted. "And I'm sorry about that, Erica. But you know what's ailing me—it's not something I wished upon myself."

"I don't blame you for falling sick, Rich. What happened to you could have happened to anyone. I had needs, darling, and I felt neglected the entire time I cared for you. I know you've suffered, but do I also need to suffer, too?"

"But you could have told me," he complained and beat his fist on the bed. "You could have been honest with me, Erica."

"I could have, yes, and I apologize for that, honey. But like I said, I was afraid you'd have said no."

"Maybe I would have said no, but then I would have thought about it. I'd like to know how you met him. Can you be honest with me about that?"

"Sure," I said and returned to the bed. "If you must know, I was having a bad day when he and I met..."

*****

"It was a Saturday in August last year when I met Terrence. I remember it like yesterday. I had dropped you off at the hospital where you needed some test work done; the doctor said he would finish with you in an hour, so I had time to burn. I went to a restaurant half a block from the hospital and sat there waiting. Tears filled my eyes at some point, and I started to cry. Terrence appeared out of nowhere and offered me a handkerchief. He sat down and asked what was bothering me. I told him about your situation. He told me to take heart, saying it wasn't the end of the world and that you'd likely pull through. He somehow got me laughing, feeling buoyant about myself. I returned to pick you up, and the doctor said you'd shown some improvement; I took it as a good sign that Terrence had made me feel optimistic regarding your health."

"Weeks passed, and I drove you back for more check-ups and went to the restaurant. I wasn't thinking about Terrence, never even thought I'd run into him again, but there he was. He said he worked for a brokerage firm, and his office was across the street, and was on his lunch break. We got to talking. He got me laughing, made me feel good about myself, and then we exchanged phone numbers."

"He and I talked later that evening while you slept. Everything sounded innocent at the time—nothing serious or overtly sexual—he was like a genuine friend. I was a near-emotional wreck then and I had nobody to talk to. You were weak much of the time while you recuperated—you couldn't have known what I was going through even if I'd told you, and then, you probably would have laughed, thinking I was comparing your problems with mine. That was how I felt, and I wanted someone to hold my hand and be like a friend to me. That turned out to be Terrence."

"I called him days later, and we decided to meet for lunch. I told him about how I was feeling and how bad I felt that you were ill. The longer we talked, the more I knew I wanted something more from him."

"Was that the first time you screwed him?"

"No," I said. "That happened days later after you'd gotten way better."

"Where did you two fuck the first time?"

*****

"It happened on a rainy Tuesday. We met for lunch, but I wanted something more; Terrence knew it, and we got into my car and drove to some quiet spot off the main highway.

We started kissing the instant I switched off the engine. Minutes later, we unclipped our seatbelt and maneuvered ourselves into the backseat."

"Terrence unzipped his pants, and I knelt beside him with my butt pressed against the side window. I sniffed his prick seconds before he whipped it out and offered it to me to suck on. Suck on it, I did. He tasted good. I wanted more of his cock, so I sucked him harder."

"His cock grew hard in my mouth. I found myself moaning like I was the happiest woman ever. I felt his fingers probing past my panties, feeling against my wet pussy. The feel of his fingers reminded me of how sex-starved I was—I'd never been so eager to fuck that rainy afternoon."

"I lifted my skirt, pulled my panties to the side, slid across his thigh, and straddled him. His prick pressed against my thigh. Terrence adjusted himself, and I helped to insert his prick inside me. His hands pawed my butt and slid my panties over my ass cheeks while I rode him. The car jerked against us—it was tough riding him in that cramped backseat—I reminded myself that next time, we would do it in his car instead."

"I worked my booty against his cock as hard as I could. I breathed against his face while we kissed. Our breathing got heavy, and the back windows got misty. But the feel of his cock inside me was incredible. I kept jerking my butt up and down and then side to side. I could feel my cunt creaming over his prick. We gasped harder the longer we fucked."

*****

"Did he cum inside you?"

"No," I answered. "We stopped before he did. I slid off him and jerked his cock till he came in my hand."

"What did you then do?" Richard asked.

"I licked his cum off my palm," I said.

"What happened next?"

"We waited until we felt better, then we drove back to the restaurant, said our goodbyes, and went our separate ways."

"And that was the start of your relationship with Terrence."

"Yes, it was," I said. "Is that all you want to know, Rich? Can we call it a night now?"

"Just one last thing, and I don't want any arguments about this: I want to meet this Terrence fellow. Good night."

He switched off his bedside light, curled under the covers with his back toward me, and fell asleep. I watched him briefly before switching off my bedside light and letting the night take me.

5

Sexually Satisfy
a Gilf with Two

I barely slept that night. My dream was populated with snapshots and reels of Terrence and I frolicking carelessly in different places where we had made love—in the backseat of my car, including his, over in his apartment, and several times we had been pressed for time and opted to fuck in some outdoor spot—once, I remember we almost got spotted by a patrolling cop at a nearby park—*talk about living dangerously!* In each dream, the foreboding shadow of Richard lurked in the background, observing us, taking notes, never intruding, but always in the shadows like a ferret, watching.

My eyes blinked open several times during the night. I turned over and heard Richard snoring on his side, oblivious to my turmoil. He wanted to meet with Terrance. He said I wasn't as smart as I thought I was. I had apparently misjudged him and slipped up somewhere, somehow. Likely, he had hired someone to follow me around. It couldn't have been any of the kids or neighbors; possibly, he'd hired someone professional, or else I'd have noticed.

My eyes opened for what felt like the fifth time, and this time, I got up and went into the bathroom to urinate. I sat on the toilet seat, thinking about whoever Richard might have hired to trail me—if he knew who Terrence was, then he wasn't lying about knowing where he lived. I wondered if it was too late to warn Terrence. But then again, what was the point when Richard wanted to meet him in person?

I washed my hands and face before returning to bed. This time, sleep did cart me off smoothly.

Morning came and I awoke. I started the day like usual: I went downstairs and performed some yoga exercises before making breakfast. Richard was outside, watering the garden and feeding the dogs. We later sat in the kitchen, as usual. I made tea for him and coffee for myself. Neither of us said anything at first; I eventually ended the silence.

"You still want to meet Terrence?"

"I do."

"What if he doesn't want to meet you?"

"I think you can do a good job persuading him," Richard suggested. "He's been here before, so getting him over shouldn't be that hard."

"Who did you hire to follow me?"

He shook his head. "That shouldn't concern you, Erica. Just talk to lover-boy Terrence and fix us a date to meet; worry about that instead."

I clamped up after that—nothing would budge Richard, and I knew better than to test him. I finished my breakfast, took his plate, including mine, and went to wash them in the sink. Richard left me and went about whatever else he was doing while I thought about what I would say to Terrence later when I called him.

I returned upstairs and took my phone with me into the bathroom. I turned the lock, sat on the toilet seat, and dialed his number. He answered as expected—it felt good hearing his voice. We made plans to meet later at noon at the restaurant across from his office.

Noon came, and I was there waiting minutes before he showed up. I was sipping white wine and wasn't in the mood to eat anything. I smiled when he entered the restaurant, and we kissed before settling into our table.

"Richard wants to meet you," I wasted no time telling him why I was there. "He knows about us," I continued. "Looks like he's known for a while."

"You told him?"

I shook my head. My hands were shaking; Terrence held them in his.

"He ain't got a gun in the house, does he?"

"No," I chuckled. "Richard wouldn't know what to do with one if he did. I'm just worried about whatever he'd want to say to you."

"It couldn't be anything worse. You think he'd want us not to see each other again?"

"Yeah. That's the only thing weighing on my mind; he'd done stuff like this before."

"With some other guy?"

"Yeah, but that was years ago. Some guy who liked giving me a good time. Richard got jealous, and I think he felt the guy wanted to steal me away from him."

Terrence leaned forward and smiled. "I'll bet it was so. Did he?"

"He did tell me once that he wanted me to leave Richard. I never would have thought of doing that, and I never told Richard, but he's got a nose for such things. Almost like he smelled a rat and made me break off from the guy."

"He had every right to do what he did; I mean your husband."

"Yeah, I guess he did. But I don't know about you. You're not like that other guy."

"Why, because I ain't told you to blow your marriage for me?"

That enticed me to laugh; the laughter was an enormous relief pill when I let it out. "You're so silly! But, yes, I guess because of that. And to think I almost would if you'd told me to."

"I was never going to," Terrence said. "It's never my business to break up marriages, and meeting you wasn't something I'd planned. Shit just happened."

"It did. But what are we going to do now?"

"How about we make do with the little good time we've got to share and worry about other stuff later? You've got someplace you want to be right now?"

"Besides coming to tell you about Richard, no. What do you have in mind?"

"Since we aren't eating, we can chill out somewhere," he said. "Over at my buddy Ken's place—you remember Ken, right? His place isn't too far from here. We can go hang out there for a while."

I did know of Ken, a best friend of his. Terrence and I have had plenty of fun at his place; I wonder if Richard's alleged spy might know of him, too. What the hell, who gives a fuck!

"Sure, let's go."

I picked up my handbag before offering him my hand. We left the restaurant, got into our separate cars, and drove to his friend's apartment. Ken's place was three blocks from the restaurant. I almost wished he wouldn't be there when we arrived, but sure as fuck, he opened the door when Terrence knocked. He wore a pair of jeans and no shirt; nothing about him looked like he was about to leave. We entered his apartment, and I hugged and kissed his cheek before asking why we hadn't visited him in a while.

"Busy, busy, man," Terrence answered. "You ain't fixing to head out soon?"

"Was playing some video game before you both got here," he said. "But you two go on and do your thing."

We left him in the living room and made for his bedroom.

Terrence shut the door while I let down my handbag from my shoulder before settling on the bed. He approached me, and my hand instinctively grabbed at his crotch. His Johnson was starting to come alive the longer I felt him.

"You don't look too happy to see me," I muttered more to his semi-erection than to Terrence.

"Take it out, and you'll see how happy it is," he replied.

I unzipped his fly, reached into the opening of his pants, grabbed his prick, and pulled it out into daylight. My lips watered as I stroked pre-cum out of his penis. My mouth welcomed him appropriately. A cat-like murmur purred through my throat as I committed to sucking him. Terrence undid his belt buckle and let his pants and pair of briefs fall down his hips. I cupped his testicles in my other hand while still jerking his girth into my mouth. His hand slid between my blouse, wanting to get at my breasts. I stopped my activity to assist him before resuming from where I had stopped.

Terrence laid his clothes on a chair before lying on the bed. It was my turn to strip, and I was in the middle of that when the door creaked, and Ken stuck his head inside. He grinned when he saw me slipping out of my panties. I would have been nervous if it had been someone else. Terrence had shared me with Ken numerous times before. His cock was as efficient as Terrence, making for a terrific combination whenever I was in the mood.

"You got done playing your games, Ken?" Terrence asked his friend.

"Nah. I've had enough PlayStation for one day."

Ken stood by the door, jerking his cock while ogling me as I discarded my final item. I got on the bed and resumed my fun with Terrence. Ken approached the bed, took my hand, and brought it to his cock. I wrapped my fingers around his hard-on and jerked his meat while slobbering on Terrence. Later, I pulled away from Terrence and offered Ken a similar blowjob appreciation. Terrence stood beside me; he and Ken flanked me, compelling me to suck them back and forth. I spate on their cocks and stroked their girth while gorging on their dicks. At one point, they both stuck their cocks into my mouth. I mumbled and blubbered with excitement as drools of spite rolled down my chin.

Ken then lay on the bed, and Terrence positioned himself behind me while I paid attention to Ken's erection. Terrence slapped my butt and muttered a remark about how big and round my butt was before inserting his cock between my vulva. I grunted and jerked forward as he rammed into me. His cock filled me incredibly; I gripped

Ken's cock tight and sucked his cock harder. I shut my eyes from the immense pleasure flooding my pussy from behind. Terrence grabbed me by my waist, grunting hard while punishing me with his girth. I couldn't simmer my exhaling moans in response to his thrusts; I couldn't help wanting more and more of him.

Terrence slapped my butt one final time before pulling away. Ken guided me to come and straddle him, which I did. I was working my hips, grinding and thrusting against his pelvis. My tits flew either way; Ken grabbed them and gave them a good squeeze. I leaned over him, groaning my pleasure while slowing my pace so he could enjoy a mouthful of my tits.

As if I thought Terrence was done, he came beside me and fingered my asshole while I bucked and rocked against Ken. I was huffing and moaning like a wild stallion. Terrence mounted me, and I stopped so he could work his prick into my anal hole.

I squeezed my eyes and gritted my teeth, neither of which stopped the searing groan that escaped my throat. My asshole felt like it had been stretched to an unbelievable size. The pain stayed with me but gradually dissipated so I could ride both men easily. It wasn't often that I enjoyed taking two cocks simultaneously; I always lived to cherish the moment.

Time seemed to run fast with no end. I had no idea how long Terrence stayed hunched over me until he pulled out and allowed Ken to have his fun. Ken got me on all fours, and he took time fucking me in both holes, banging away at my mature booty until he pulled out and squirted his load down my throat.

6

Can a Gilf Strike Black?

Ken showered, changed into a fresh pair of clothes, and then left the apartment for Terrence and me to continue our fun. Terrence wasn't in a hurry to return to work. He mentioned today was supposed to be his day off, and he had visited the office to sign off on some paperwork he had previously neglected on his desk.

Something then occurred to me that made me sit upright. Ken was surprised when I left the bed and rushed out of the room. Ken asked what the matter was, but I didn't stop until I got to the living room and peeked out the window curtains. Ken's window had a view of the western section of the apartment building's parking lot; the parking lot was in an L-shaped design that took up a quarter of the entire compound. Several cars were there (I picked out mine and Ken's beside each other), but I was looking for any vehicle that looked incongruous with the neighborhood. Anything inconspicuous.

Ken appeared beside me and peeked past the curtains, trying to figure out whatever I was observing.

"You're turning paranoid, you know," he remarked with a chuckle.

"I'm sorry, babe. But I know Richard has got somebody out there following me around," I said. "What are the chances that I return home and he already knows I'm here?"

"At least then he'd know your ass was here, telling me about having a sit-down with him," Ken said. "Or ain't that why you called so we could see today?"

"That's part of it," I admitted, smiling as I let the curtain fall back to its place. "But not all of it."

"Oh yeah? What's the other part you're not telling me?"

"You ought to know, silly you." I came into his arms and kissed him. "I missed you so much. Being away from you eats at my mind a lot."

"Then how about we continue from where we left off," he suggested. "Unless you're hurrying to get back to your man."

Terrence wrapped his arms around me and squeezed my butt while we stayed locked in a passionate kiss. I led him to a couch. He sat down while I knelt before his open legs and worked his cock into my mouth. I sucked him harder and worked as much vigor into my output; I slid his penis between my big pair of tits, taking pleasure in the tantalizing friction of pre-cum squirting on my torso before returning to sucking his girth. It was my wish to empty his balls so he wouldn't have enough strength if any of his other girlfriends came to enjoy their share. As for me, I would soon return home to my unexcited married life; I needed to have as much fun to remember him later when in bed beside Richard.

I came to my feet and offered Ken my hand as I bestraddled his pelvis. I adjusted my thighs for him to introduce his prick between my labia lips. My butt settled on his shaft the instant he entered me, and I sighed in ecstasy—this was ten times better than carrying out yoga exercises; riding Ken's cock was the best knock-out drug I could ingest any day.

My pelvis muscles did a majority of the work, tumbling and grinding my booty on Ken's prick while he smacked and caressed my lush booty. He gripped my ass cheeks and worked his thighs, striving to match my tempo. My breathing flowed through my nostrils and out of my mouth as our workout switched into high gear. I wrapped my arms around his shoulder and shoved my breasts against his torso. Ken lowered himself to suck my tits while I upped my riding pace.

My booty continued to smack hard on his thighs.

The smacking noise drove me buck-wild, combined with his cock stretching my cunt; it invigorated me to grind harder.

Ken slid his hands under my thigh and stopped to lift himself off the couch. He tottered briefly before coming to his feet and hitched me further into his grip to start working his pelvis against me. His cock slid deeper inside my cunt; I responded by whimpering louder while raking my nails across his shoulders. Ken turned around and lowered me onto the couch. He propped my feet over his shoulder, balanced his knee beside my thigh, and got to fucking me hard and deep. His cock jammed further into my womb; my pussy climaxed faster than usual.

Ken later turned me over on my knees and fucked me anally. I grabbed the couch's headrest, and my chin brushed roughly against the fabric as I whimpered and hollered from the brash pounding I received. Ken hunched over me, his hands gripped my waist, and his fingers dug into my flesh as he thrust the length of his girth into my cunt. He gasped and breathed against my neck. I turned my face to the side, and he attempted to kiss me. His didn't lessen his pace—he was giving me everything he bore in his arsenal of fucking.

I screamed when he thrust deep into me and stayed there for several seconds before pulling out. He was already leaking cum when I turned around, grabbed his prick, and let him gush his seed down my windpipe. It was unfortunate because I would have preferred if he had climaxed inside me.

*****

I left the apartment alone; I didn't want to risk my follower (if he was out there) getting further evidence of my adultery to share with Richard. I tried to appear inconspicuous as I exited the building and strolled to my car. I didn't recognize the black old-school Cadillac Sedan parked to my passenger side—I could have sworn it wasn't there when we first arrived—and I paid it no mind as I settled into my vehicle. It wasn't until a black man appeared on the driver's side and hissed at me to catch my attention. I was about to key in my ignition when I turned and was startled by the man staring at me.

"How come you're out here alone? Where's your lover, Ken?"

I was stunned for words; seconds passed before I could find my voice.

"Excuse me, who are you?"

"You're heading for home right now, aren't you?" He said. "Your husband wants to know how much time since you've been gone. You reckon I should tell him?"

"Who the…who the fuck are you?" I snapped.

"Figured you'd ask." He offered me a business card bearing his name and the business he was into. I'd finally met the man who Richard appointed to follow me around. "Thaddeus Black, private investigator, at your service," he smiled.

*****

I arrived home more than an hour later. I checked myself in my mirror to ensure everything was perfect before leaving the car. Richard was in the den drinking a beer while watching a football game.

"You finally came home," he said after I entered the living room. "Was wondering what's kept you."

"You were worried I wasn't coming home?"

"Why would I ever, hon? I knew you'd be home, just didn't know when or what's kept you since. How was Terrence? Did you send my love?"

"If that's your way of being sarcastic, it's not working. And yes, I did meet with Terrence and told him about you wanting to meet him. He said he'll be free this Saturday."

"Saturday; that's four days away. You couldn't convince him to drop by sooner?"

"He said he's going to be busy through the week with work."

"Oh, how unfortunate. That means you aren't going out to see him until then, are you?"

"No, I'm not."

I made for the stairs but stopped when Richard called my name.

"You didn't happen to fuck him while you were with him today, did you, Erica? Best tell me if you did."

I turned toward him; Richard left his chair and approached me. "Why bother asking me that? Surely, you can find that out for yourself from whoever you've got following me."

"I certainly can, but I'd like it from the horse's mouth. Did you screw him today, yes or no?"

"I'm not going to bother giving you an answer to that question, Richard. Take any guess you'd like."

"Okay, let's say you had sex with him, and I'm not upset if you did. Do tell me one thing, did he cum in you?"

To answer his question, I lifted my skirt, unabashedly revealing my panties, and said, "Why don't you come and insert your finger right into my cunt. See if some fluid pours out."

Richard shook his head. "I guess you've proven your point, Erica. Come Saturday, I'll ask him myself."

"You do that, Rich," I said, lowering my skirt and then headed up the stairs. "In the meantime, I'm going to catch an hour's worth of sleep, maybe even two."

Richard didn't have a comeback to that and I was glad he didn't as I went upstairs to the bedroom. I figured he would be on his phone, calling his private investigator to find out whatever he could about my time spent with

Terrence. I smiled to myself, knowing already what Thaddeus would inform him.

It feels good to have the upper hand for once, I thought as I slammed the bedroom door behind me.

7

What Happens When a Gilf Goes Private

I got out of my car and the private investigator opened his passenger door for me to enter. I slid inside, shut his door, gave him a sassy look, and said, "So, what now?"

"I'm going to come clean with you, Erica," he said. "Your husband contacted me three weeks ago to tail you. He figured his woman was out doing some things she ought not be doing, and he wanted verifiable proof in case he needed to take you to the cleaners, or the other way around."

This was shocking news and I took it as such. "Richard was thinking about divorcing me?"

Thaddeus Black nodded. "I don't know if he ain't anymore—I usually don't like getting into my clients' heads to know what they want to do about stuff they pay me to do. Often, it's like watching people strolling along the edge of a high-rise. What I sometimes do is suggest ways and means of talking them down, but that's if they choose to listen. I've been doing this business for a long time, and I hate to imagine marriages ending because of me snooping around."

"A private investigator with a conscience," I remarked snidely. "Never thought I'd encountered one before."

"Call it whatever you want; it's a dirty game, sure, but somebody's got to do it."

"All right then," I adjusted myself in his seat. "So, you've been following me around for the past three weeks, and you've given Richard plenty of material to hang me with. How come he's still got you stuck on my ass?"

"I've got to admit, you've got a lovely fine ass," he grinned. "Having watched you and your man upstairs together, I can tell you know how to work it."

I frowned. "Am I supposed to be flattered by that? Is that a compliment, or are you being rude?"

"I always compliment fine things, and you're one fine-ass, gorgeous Gilf if ever I'd seen one."

Gilf. There goes that word again.

That raised a smile on my face, and it got me to relax a bit.

"What do you want, Mr. Thaddeus Black?"

"Please, call me Thad; everybody does. What I want is what you want. You don't want your husband divorcing you, and the last thing you want is someone like me tailing your fine ass around, right?"

"Right."

"I honestly don't want none of that either. So, how about we compromise; I'll do my best to deflect your husband off thinking about ending things with you, and you and your lover-boy can carry on without me interrupting your thing. How does that sound?"

I nodded, smiling inwardly. "I'm listening."

"You're heading home right now, and your husband's gonna call later, asking if I noticed you doing anything you shouldn't. He knows you're out there meeting with Terrence. He wants to know if you both had fun—that's what gets him upset—and I'm gonna tell him the opposite."

"He's going to believe you as opposed to me telling him no?"

"You ought to know your husband by now, Erica. Why else would I be out here chasing after you if he couldn't get the truth from you?"

"Okay, I see your point, and though I hate admitting this, I'm grateful. But what would you want in return? Money?"

He laughed. "Your man's got that part covered. What I want is something else."

His voice sounded silky and he laid his hand on my thigh and began caressing me; that was all I needed to know.

"Maybe you can show me what a sexy Gilf you are, and if you're nice to me, then we can be excellent friends."

"Is this something you do with female clients? Is this your way of taking undue advantage of me?"

"I ain't taking advantage of anything that ain't already been gotten. You can leave if you want, and won't see me bugging you again. You won't even catch me watching you because I'm too good not to get caught. I'm simply making you an exchange here. It's up to you if you want to take it or not. And you'd better decide soon before your man upstairs comes out and finds us talking."

I had almost forgotten where I was when he said that. He was right: Terrence could leave the building right now, find me sitting in this stranger's car, and wonder what we're about.

"Is there someplace we can go?"

Thad smiled. "Sure," he said.

I returned to my car and followed the private investigator as we drove out of the parking grounds. I had no idea where he was taking me. I figured I'd do as he wanted, and hopefully, he would help deflect whatever demented thought Richard had cooking for me. I couldn't believe how absent-minded I'd been regarding everything I'd been doing up until that moment, stuff that could inevitably lead to the dissolution of my marriage. Divorce was never what I wanted, especially once my kids realized why. Richard would love nothing more than to humiliate me that way.

With this so-called private investigator, Thaddeus Black, it was sex he wanted; well, then, that was what he was going to fucking get.

Thad hadn't mentioned where we were going when he told me to return to my car and follow him. I figured we were heading someplace far and worried I wouldn't be home for a while; Richard hadn't called me. He didn't care or figured he would hear best from his investigator about whatever I'd been doing.

We drove across town, headed toward the riverside, and then, to my surprise, followed Thaddeus into a decrepit-looking alleyway. He stopped his car, and I did the same behind him and got out. He came from his driver's side and gestured at me to get into the backseat with him.

"Don't tell me this is where you reside," I said as I slid inside.

"Nah, babe. That might be for next time; this would do for a rest stop."

He got in and shut his door. "Don't worry about anyone finding us; hardly anyone comes by here."

"You can guarantee that?"

"Nope," he laughed and got busy unzipping his fly. "But once you put your mouth to this, everything's gonna feel just right."

Thad extracted his semi-turgid erection, wanting me to be impressed by his girth, before undoing his belt buckle. I sure was impressed as I wrapped my hand around his shaft and began jerking him. I adjusted my frame before lowering my head down his crotch. Two pulls of my mouth were all it took for him to grow to full erection. Thad moaned responsively; he sneaked his hand into my blouse to caress my tits. My nipples were hard, whether from sucking his cock or my earlier sex with Terrence. I wasn't thinking about Terrence then, nor did Richard, my husband, play in my mind.

I was aroused, hooked, and attracted to worshipping the black cock before me. That was all I cared about.

I closed my eyes, inhaling his musky, arousing smell emanating from his crotch while his cock stretched my jawline. My other hand pulled his pants downward so I could reach underneath to grasp his testicles. Thad pulled my skirt over my backside to squeeze my fleshy butt. Streams of saliva dribbled out of my mouth the longer I played with his cock. The longer I sucked him, the more enticed I was not to stop. Even though I knew it was wrong, I almost didn't seem to care if someone happened by and caught us.

"Damn, babe. You are one solid mature bitch, you sure are," Thad groaned while stroking my hair. "I'll bet this is why you can't stay away from your boyfriend. You're so addicted to his cock, ain't you?"

"I sure am," I replied.

"Good. 'Cos you're gonna add me to the list. I'm gonna want next on this Gilf pussy you have here. Come here, let me get some of that pink snatch under your skirt."

I applied my lips to one final drag before letting go of his prick. I glanced around to ensure the coast was clear before mounting him. He slid my panties over my butt and pressed his prick's head against my vulva. I should have stopped to reflect upon what I was about to do. I was about to have sex with a stranger, which seemed somewhat dangerous. I had no idea how safe or clean he was, or if I should be doing this…but somehow, neither of those red flags made a dent in my head as I impaled myself on his prick.

It felt good.

No, it felt *incredibly fantastic!*

My pussy muscles clenched upon receiving his prick, and my pelvis began to ride him.

*****

My eyes opened when I heard a door slam shut. I realized I was back in my home, in my bedroom, and I instantly panicked as it felt like I had been "caught doing something I shouldn't be doing.

Richard had entered the room and dropped something on the table before entering the bathroom. He couldn't see what I was doing under the covers, which I was grateful he didn't, or he would have seen my hand locked between my thighs while I recalled the sex I had with his investigator. I closed my eyes, pretending to be asleep, while listening to the noise he made in the bathroom. There was a toilet flushing noise, and then Richard came out. He stood there momentarily, seeming undecided about what to do, before leaving the room. I smiled and wondered if he had called Thaddeus to find out more.

Likely, he had.

8

A Gilf's Lover Comes Knocking at the Front Door

Terrence called me on Friday evening, letting me know he would arrive at my front door around 11:00 a.m. He inquired again if I was honest about Richard not having a gun. I told him to stop being ridiculous. I knew he was trying to make light of the situation, and I was grateful for the poor attempt at humor. The pleasant feeling stayed with me when I told Richard what time Terrence would be coming before falling asleep.

Morning arrived, and I was up and out of bed before my alarm clock sounded off. I went downstairs to sit alone in the living room to meditate through my worries. I'd wanted to be alone but I ended up waking Polly, my two-year-old Boxer dog, who came and stretched beside my thigh. Richard hadn't told me what he intended to say to Terrence. He didn't appear to be seething with anger, but even that wasn't comforting. Richard knew how to mask his feelings, especially from me, whenever he wanted. There was nothing I could have said to Terrence to prepare him for his upcoming encounter. Hopefully, it will be over and done quickly.

I felt helpless and I despised the feeling. I despised feeling torn between wanting my lover and maintaining my marriage. Polly whined and nuzzled against my thigh for attention; I absently petted her while fighting to calm my nerves. Morning sunlight streamed past the window curtains. I should be doing some yoga, but today was an outright exception. Instead of yoga, I went to the kitchen to brew coffee, anything to cure my nervousness. Polly trailed behind me, demanding a doggie treat, which I inevitably gave her. I thought through the day's outcome while waiting for my water to heat up.

The worst case scenario was picturing Richard cursing Terrence out, demanding we quit our interaction or I risk getting divorce papers from him. That was the most pertinent outcome that echoed in my mind as I grabbed a mug out of a cabinet drawer and filled it with hot water.

I remained in the kitchen even after I was done with my coffee, petting my dog while observing the sunrise beyond the crown of trees behind our yard. Richard came to join me later, grunting with each step. His features looked pale and sallow like he had exerted himself from getting up from bed.

"How are you?" I asked.

"Great, except I feel like a rhino ran over me last night. You got more of that coffee around?"

"Yeah, sure." I made him a cup while he sat at the table and played with Polly; her other sibling, Tom, a German Shepard, was yet to come awake. Tom was Richard's favorite. I set about making breakfast while Richard enjoyed his coffee. It wasn't long before Tom appeared in the room, and both dogs stretched on the floor, awaiting our beck and call.

"What's your day going to be like?" Richard asked.

"I was thinking about getting my hair done, but that can wait. I've got to make some floral arrangements for my friend, Sarah; her daughter's getting married soon, and she wants me around to help her with things."

"You won't want to stick around for your lover-boy when he gets here?"

"I figured you wouldn't want me around for that."

"You can stay for his sake; wouldn't be fair if you're not around to welcome him. Maybe you can hold his hand if you want."

"Are you trying to aggravate me as you've done already? You want to keep rubbing it into my face and now want to do it in front of him, is that it?"

"No, that's not it. I'm merely being realistic, Erica. He's your lover, and it won't look good if you're not around. You can leave if you want, but I think it'd be great if you were here. That's up to you."

"I'll give it some thought," I replied and continued with my meal.

"Unless you're going to call him not to show," he smirked. "Not that I'd blame you if you did that either."

I gave him a cold look and then returned to finishing my meal.

I went upstairs to tidy up the bedroom before taking a shower. I didn't bother calling Terrence; I wouldn't give Richard the satisfaction of letting him cower me to mental submission.

I had no idea when I dozed off. The noise of my ringing phone stirred me awake, and it was Terrence calling to let me know he was close to my driveway. I left the bed and washed my face in the bathroom before rushing downstairs.

Richard wasn't in the living room, to my surprise. The doorbell rang, and I opened the door and welcomed Terrence into my home. He looked casual, good-looking, and sharp in his white shirt and gray jacket; I pulled him in for a hug, inhaling his aftershave.

"You smell good, babe," he said.

"You look handsome and good to eat," I replied cheekily, unable to hide my blush. "I kept praying for you not to show."

"Looks like those went unanswered. Where's your man? Let's get this over and done with here."

"Hi, Terrence." We both turned to see Richard enter the living room from the door leading to his library; I had neglected to think he might be there. "I'm so glad you made it over."

Richard approached, and he shook hands with Terrence. He was as amiable as ever.

"I hope it wasn't too much for you to accept my invitation," he said.

"You wanted me to come, so I did," Terrence shrugged. "Whatever reason you had in mind."

"Erica and I have been talking about you. It seemed only fair that she introduced me to the fellow who's been screwing her behind my back this entire time. Come in, let's have a seat. Let Erica get us something to drink. You care for a beer, soda, or something stronger?"

"A glass of water will do just fine."

"What about you, darling?" I asked Richard.

"I can use a beer," he answered.

Richard led Terrence to the living room while I went to get the drinks. I returned minutes later with their separate orders. They thanked me for the service. I wanted to leave, but Richard eyed me, indicating he wanted me to stick around, so I sat across from them, feeling displaced in their presence.

"You know why I invited you here, Terrence. I'm not going to lie to you, I was damn near ballistic when I first found out about you and my wife. You knew she was married when you first met her, right?"

"Sure, I did."

"And that never deterred you from wanting to spend fun time with her?"

"I wouldn't be here if it did," Terrence retorted.

"No, I didn't think that either," Richard agreed. "Nothing would please me more than telling you I don't want to see you having anything to do with her anymore. I reckon you figured that's something I have in mind to tell you."

Terrence nodded and clasped his hands between his knees. He appeared uneasy like he couldn't wait for Richard to conclude his talk so he could leave. I, too, was getting frustrated and wanted the whole thing to end. I almost wanted to apologize to Terrence for wasting his time like this.

"I'd like to watch you have sex with her," Richard said to my astonishment. "I'd like to know how good you are at fucking my Erica than I'd presume you do."

Terrence looked at me like he wanted to ensure he hadn't heard wrong. I looked at him, equally stunned; several seconds passed before he could respond.

"Are you sure about what I just heard you say?"

"You heard right," said Richard. "Erica has had boyfriends before—I'll bet she's mentioned that to you. She wouldn't have stuck with you this long if you weren't fucking her good. I'd like to see you two together in bed to judge for myself."

Terrence was again speechless and looked at me again, to which I attempted to communicate with my eyes to let him know I had nothing to do with what Richard was saying. Richard, for his part, appeared to take amused delight in our confusion as he sat back and sipped his beer.

"You're serious?" Terrence asked.

"I certainly am serious," Richard boldly replied, then turned to me and said, "Erica, why not come sit beside your man here? No need to be shy since we're friends here. Come on."

I left where I was sitting and came to sit beside Terrence, feeling like a schoolgirl awaiting punishment. I laid my hand on his thigh for warmth and solace; my mind was confused about what my husband was about.

"Come on, you can do better than that, can't you, hon?" Richard gestured at me to dig in closer to Terrence. "Go ahead, give him a kiss. Quit acting like you ain't kissed him before."

"This isn't funny, Rich," I said. "Whatever type of humor this is, I'd like you to cut it out right now."

"Do I look like I'm laughing, Erica—I'm dead serious like a heart attack here. I want you two to have sex right now, if possible. You can start here or take things upstairs, I don't mind. I want you to show me how bad you want this."

I tensely sat there, confounded in disbelief. I probably would have acted differently and told him to fuck off were it not for Terrence, who was holding my hand and caressing it. I turned to him, about to say something, but Terrence planted his lips to mine and kissed me. It took seconds for me to respond to his kiss. The feel of his tongue sliding between my lips automatically transported me to another world, where there were only the two of us, and Richard was nowhere in sight to intrude. It wasn't easy at first, and I struggled to control my urges. My mind was still reeling with the confusion of believing my husband, but Terrence had his arm around me, preventing me from pulling away. He assumed my nervousness was inclining me toward wanting to stop. But why should I ever? It wasn't like I hadn't had sex with other men in Richard's presence before, even though that was years ago. Suddenly, the thought of attempting this felt like a new experience.

At some point, I extracted my lips from Terrence and muttered, "We shouldn't be doing this. Not like this in front of him."

"If not now, then when?" He replied.

His words were honest, and as I was about to counter, he kissed me fiercely, which sealed the deal between us.

9

Fucking a Gilf While Hubby Watches

I assisted Terrence out of his gray jacket and folded it on a chair. There was a sudden commotion in the kitchen, and we looked in that direction, but Richard laughed when he saw it was Polly and Tom seemingly squabbling like siblings over one of Polly's toys.

"Don't tell me you two can't simply get along," Richard chuckled as he wrenched the toy from the locked jaw of both dogs. "Come on, you two. Let's get you both a treat or two." He turned to us and said, "You can both carry on without me; I'll be back in a bit."

I waited until Richard left the room, taking both dogs with him, then turned to Terrence, "Are you sure you want to go ahead with this?"

"We're doing it already," Terrence answered as he unbuttoned his shirt. "Let's not argue about it anymore; bring that fine ass of yours back here," he tapped the side of the sofa I'd previously occupied beside him.

"Let's take things upstairs instead," I helped him to his feet. My blood was stirring, producing a comforting warmth within myself; I perceived my cheeks glowing crimson. "If this is what Richard wants, let's give him a better show."

"Now you're talking, babe."

Terrence smacked my butt and gave it a loving caress as we made for the stairs.

We were halfway into enjoying ourselves in the bedroom when Richard came looking for us. Terrence was slumped on a chair beside the bed with his jeans and pair of briefs halfway down his thighs while I knelt before him, gorging myself on his cock. We were unconcerned about Richard's presence as he shut the door and mentioned that he had tied the dogs to prevent them from following him. My concentration was on pleasuring my lover. Richard was right about his assessment in figuring I'd made love to Terrence here before. He probably knew Terrence visited me during my last babysitting venture. We had been in such a hurry that day I'd likely slipped up when I shouldn't have. There was no hurry this time, and I felt somewhat content that Richard was seeing for himself what I had been enjoying behind his back. Hopefully, it would jog his memory to recall the long-ago period he witnessed me in bed with another man.

My blouse was open, and my other hand was busy caressing my tits; Terrence gasped from my effort while busying himself with caressing my hair. We could have been back at his place; it was so soothing that I lied to myself about where I was so I didn't lose the fantasy playing in my head.

I stroked his cock with loving care while ingesting his shaft, enjoying the turgid feel of his girth as he stretched my mouth wide. A minute later, I rose to my feet, lifted my skirt, and settled on his crotch. I caressed Terrence's shoulders while we locked in a deep, passionate kiss. His hands caressed my backside down to squeezing my butt. He lifted my skirt to grab at my flesh. His fingers slid past my panties and started rubbing against my vulva, eliciting enormous excitement inside me.

I had no idea what Richard was doing while he watched us. I took a moment to glance over my shoulders at him and was disappointed that he wasn't masturbating to our activity; perhaps he was waiting for us to get started on the main action.

I adjusted myself on top of him, though there was little room for me, so I lifted myself and spread my legs over the chair's armrests. A shiver ran through me, and I gasped as Terrence rummaged his fingers inside my pussy, making me further wet with anticipation. His other hand was stroking his cock against my crotch; I lifted myself further to enable him to insert the tip inside me. The shiver spread across my body as I came down on him while tightening my grip around his shoulders.

"Give it to me, babe," I moaned and gritted my teeth as I felt his shaft pierce my cunt further. "Ohh, babe, don't stop!"

My body tensed as my butt lingered inches from his crotch. Terrence had firm control over my body. His fingers dug into my buttocks as he responded by jerking his thighs and pelvis, wanting to meet me halfway. I was wracked by a tingling sensation spreading across my womb. The sensation felt like a forest fire engulfing my innards, compelling me to tense against his frame. This shouldn't be occurring like this—it wasn't like I hadn't made love to

Terrence plenty of times to not have become comfortable with his erection inside me, but this time felt completely different. Perhaps it's because I was having sex under some slight duress with my husband in the room observing us. No way would I have talked myself into wanting sex now if Terrence hadn't cut through my protest minutes ago. This felt like a release of inner turmoil unleashing out of me. I waited for the sensation to simmer somewhat before prodding my body to enjoy the moment.

I interlocked my fingers behind Terrence's neck and clenched my pussy muscles each time he rammed into me. I exhaled my grunts in near sync with his breathing against my face. The way he squeezed his eyes let me know I was getting through to him. I got to jerking my booty forward while still keeping up with my pussy clenching.

Terrence wrapped his arms around my back and held me tight, grunting as he struggled to pull himself to his feet. I held him tight as he carted me off my feet and immediately linked my ankles behind his butt. Terrence lifted me higher, and I felt my stomach muscles clench as he began pounding me harder while I hung onto him. My eyes stayed shut, but my body surrendered to his ramming power as he aggressively shot his prick inside me. My cries went wild with lust; I heard myself screaming aloud his name, demanding more of him, unable to contain myself. Terrence grunted fiercely against me; I leaned closer to taste the river of sweat dripping down his chin.

Terrence firmly gripped my butt and continued jerking me against his pelvis while slamming into me. He kissed me one last time before staggering toward the bed and dropped me on it. I almost expected him to be on top of me; instead, he dropped to his knees, held my legs apart, and brought his head down my crotch. I flung my head either way, whimpering aloud while caressing his shoulders. He shoved his tongue into my vagina, probing and digging through the nectar of my pussy like he was slurping up ice cream. My thighs jerked and spasmed uncontrollably like I was having a searing climatic episode, which I was, but I barely thought of it. The orgasm shot me into the stars, and I could do nothing but tense while it consumed me entirely. I was busy mouthing wild, crazy gibberish while my body struggled to maintain its poise.

Terrence then came up for air. I reached for him and pulled him toward me.

"I want you, babe," I groaned as I kissed him. "I fucking want you inside me!"

There was only Terrence and me in the room. Richard was standing two feet from the bed, but he might as well have been on Mars.

I was scrubbing myself in the bathroom while Terrence talked with Richard. Richard had insisted I not be around for it, so I opted to take a long shower. I wasn't worried as I stood under the shower spray, letting water splash on my face, torso, and backside. Whatever the outcome of their discussion, what mattered most was the enjoyable sex I just had with Terrence. The sex made me feel surprisingly young with myself. I couldn't wait to tell my friend Sarah about everything. She's the only one I trust with my secrets, though it's been a while since I kept her abreast of things.

After what felt like a long and luxuriating bath, I turned off the shower and waited for some of the water to run down my body before stepping out of the stall with my towel in hand. I leaned against the door but heard nothing that sounded like people talking. I opened the door and saw the bedroom empty. They had possibly taken things downstairs, I figured, as I dried my body before putting on some lotion.

A half-hour later, I put on a new pair of clothes and bounded out of the room. The smile left my lips when I went downstairs and found Richard playing with the dogs in the living room while watching a game on TV; Terrence wasn't anywhere—that made my heart sink.

"There you are," said Richard. "Was wondering when you were going to come out of the shower."

"What happened to Terrence?"

"He left. He said he had some persons he needed to see, but he'll call you later."

I went to peer out the window facing the driveway but saw no sight of Terrence's car. "Has it been long since he left?"

"The dust outside hasn't settled since he took off. But not that you need to bother since you'll be seeing him again."

That stopped me, and I turned to look at him. "Are you serious?"

Richard said nothing but continued to pet the dogs. I stood there waiting for some response that didn't seem forthcoming.

"What did you and him talk about?"

Richard looked somewhat irritated with my question. "He told me how he enjoys being with you, and I told him how much I appreciated his honesty as long as he doesn't attempt to steal you from me. Anyway, how about we get the dogs something to eat."

That was how the conversation ended, so abruptly that I was baffled about everything that occurred aside from the fun sex with Terrence. Richard didn't mention his name for the rest of the day, and I decided not to tempt fate by bothering him about the subject.

10

Two Horny Gilfs
Trading Secrets

"That's the way things are right now," I said with an accomplished grin. "What do you think?"

Sarah, my dear friend, looked amazed like she couldn't believe everything I had told her. I felt like saying more but couldn't think of what else to add. Instead, I sipped my glass of cherry wine while reviewing everything I had narrated. It sounded outrageous as I reflected on the dilemma in my life lately, giving myself a quick recap. I had been cheating on my husband for months, unaware of him finding out, and then he'd confronted me about my adultery, demanded I invite my lover over for a weird meet-and-greet, and suggested we have sex while he watched. It was confounding to believe everything that had occurred within several days; it was outlandish to believe. Should a Hollywood executive ever contact me with the intention of turning my story into a celluloid drama, I wonder how audiences would take it. Would anyone want to agree with a married woman in her mature age—*a Gilf*—cheating on her husband? That story would likely end with people hurling rotten tomatoes at me.

The part that's not concluded is how the story would end.

"Are you going to sit there and gawk at me, or are you going to say something?" I asked my friend impatiently.

"No bullshit, Erica, this stuff happened to you," she asked. "Between you, Richard, and this other guy, Terrence… that's his name, right?"

"Yes, Terrence. You don't seem shocked by everything."

"I am shocked," Sarah replied. "Shocked that you've got this secret dalliance going on this entire time and never shared it with me. But I'm more shocked at how Richard has responded to everything, that you'd be out doing this without him knowing."

"Apparently, he knew. I don't know how I slipped up or how long he knew, and I'll admit I was wrong not telling him. But you know why."

"You're worried he'd want you to call the whole thing off."

"Yes."

"And he didn't blow a fuse when he confronted you that night?"

"I almost expected he would, but he didn't. He was calm and self-assured, and it was awkward as it was scary."

We shut down our talking when we heard the front door open and some people waltzed into the house. It was Sarah's daughter, Gail, in the company of two of her friends. They were laughing about something but stopped when they saw us in the living room. The three young women entered the living room, and I hugged Gail and told her I was happy about her upcoming wedding. She thanked me and had a quick talk with her mom before going upstairs with her friends, hurrying to catch up. Sarah had a wistful smile about herself as she settled back in her chair and leaned closer.

"They sure grow older fast, don't you think?"

"Yeah, they do," I replied wistfully. "You should see my kids. It's tough knowing they're grown up and don't need me for almost nothing anymore."

"Except when they need someone to babysit?"

I shrugged. "It's a chore I'm content to enjoy—I get to have fun with my grandkids—it's way better than sitting at home knitting sweaters and watching reality TV."

Sarah laughed and refilled her glass. "If they've gotten older, then that means we've gotten way older, too."

Sarah and I have been friends for ages. She is godmother to my daughter as I am to hers; we perceived ourselves as sisters separated at birth who somehow found each other and have stayed close. She was a year older than me, but age had yet to bend her to its will. Sarah was easy-going and charming to be around, and like me, she had her secrets, which she shared with her husband, though it was something we were both privy about.

She gestured at me to come with her and to take my glass along. She opened a side door that opened into a patio, and we went to inspect her little rose garden plantation beside the house. We were out of earshot of anyone wanting to listen to our conversation. Sarah turned on a water hose and set about watering her flowers while holding court with me. It was the middle of the morning, and the day's heat was starting to kick into high gear; I could feel beads of sweat popping around my neck and armpit the longer we stood in her garden.

"What's the sex like with your lover, Terrence?"

"It's been terrific," I said. "Beyond anything I ever want."

"Aaron and I were recently talking about getting you and Richard involved again," she said. "We've thought of organizing a swingers party with several friends, but he wants to see about getting Richard involved again."

"That's going to be tough. Richard hasn't fooled around with me in years, and with his condition, I doubt he's ever going to again."

Sarah looked at me. "So, he's okay with you fooling around with Terrence now that he's seen you two together?"

"I guess," I shrugged my shoulders simultaneously when I said that. "But it's hard to know if he's been reluctant about it. What he doesn't know is I've got some help involved."

"What do you mean?"

My phone emitted a *Beep-Beep* noise that was a note reminder of some business I had to take care of today. "Excuse me," I said and dialed a number. I spoke briefly, telling the person I was on my way before ending the call. "That's who I need to go and see about right now. You're welcome to come along unless you want to keep watering your plants all day."

"You haven't told me who you're going to see."

"It's the guy Richard set up to spy on me. He's a private eye, sort of, and lives in the city. I've got an appointment with him today."

"You're going to be fine seeing him all by yourself?"

"You can come along if you want. Unless you want to keep watering those," I gestured at her flowers.

Sarah considered the invite before putting away the hose with barely a thought and then joining me. "Ain't no fun sitting in that big house doing nothing but listening to my daughter scramble about with her friends. Where are we going?"

"The first thing you need to do is change," I said. "And then, we're heading to the city."

We returned to the main house and I sat in the living room while Sarah went upstairs to change her attire. I was thinking about my meeting with the P.I. and how it was going to go when I heard footsteps enter the room. I was startled when I saw Gail giving me a quizzical look like she had caught me doing something I ought not be doing.

"Oh, it's you, Gail. What about your friends?"

"They left a while ago. I thought my mom was here."

"She went upstairs to get something," I said.

"You two are going somewhere?"

"Yes, we're going to see a friend."

Gail advanced further into the room, standing across from me, looking at me like a lawyer would at a criminal.

"Would that happen to be a special type of friend?"

"What?"

"Aunty Erica, I know what my parents are into—their so-called dark hobby. I know they've tried their best to keep it a secret. Mom thinks I'm so godly-innocent when I'm not. I've heard her talk about you and the wild stuff you both used to do."

I was speechless and was trying to calculate if Gail was being real: had she been sneaking around, listening in on her parents, or did she somehow catch wind of my conversation with Sarah and decided to confront me about it? That would be the better option than facing her mom…but how was I to know?

"That's absurd, Gail," I replied. "There's no way you'd know the things your mom is about."

Gail glanced toward the doorway for a moment, and I, too, looked with her like I suspected Sarah was about to appear, but nobody came, and then she turned to me.

"I know she loves sex as much as she loves food," she said. "I know she and Dad have had men over here late into the night in the basement while I pretended to be asleep. I've even heard her with men in her bedroom having sex— or, to put it more bluntly—fucking her. And usually, they're always black men. I can go on and on about the times they've invited you and Uncle Richard over."

That was as far as she got as suddenly she stopped once we heard footsteps coming down the stairs. Gail became all charm and innocence once Sarah entered the room, looking pretty and casual in a cream blouse and jeans. Sarah was slightly startled seeing her but quickly mellowed as her daughter came and kissed her cheek.

"I never knew you were around. What happened to your friends?"

"Monica and Jessy had places they needed to be," said Gail. "I'll be out to visit them later. I thought I'd come and say hello to Aunt Erica. You two are taking off?"

"Yeah, I've been indoors all day and need to catch some air. Your dad ought to be home in the next hour or two—he said he won't be working late today. I should be home by then." Sarah turned to me and said, "Come on, Erica, are we leaving or what?"

"Sure." I grabbed my handbag and came after her. I held eye contact with Gail, and she made a slight gesture with her hand that said, we'll talk more later.

I had a funny feeling about what sort of talk that would be about.

*****

We drove in my car; it was more economical than driving separately. Sarah wound her window down halfway to enjoy the breeze wafting through. I turned my radio to a country music station, and Sarah approved the music choice.

The thought lingered in my head as I drove into the city about confronting Sarah with my little chat with her daughter before leaving her house. Gail was weeks away from getting married. I have met her soon-to-be husband, a handsome, bright fellow who came from old money. He and Gail met in college and have stuck together years since; he was a fine gentleman, and I assumed he would make for an ideal husband to her. Who was I to know all this time that Gail harbored illicit thoughts nearly the same as her parents? What would Sarah think if she found out her daughter wasn't so keenly naive as she figured she was this entire time?

"You looking forward to being a grandmother?" I asked.

"I don't know," Sarah mused while running her fingers through her hair, absorbing the scenery of the neighborhood we drove past. "If you're used to it, then I will, too. A part of me has been looking forward to this happening."

"What about the other part?"

"That's the part I can't figure out," she sighed. "The house will feel a lot empty once Gail leaves—something she should have done long ago. I guess that's what Aaron and I have always wanted—plenty of time to enjoy our sexual fun, know what I mean? But I don't know what it will look like when it comes. Does that make any sense?"

"You'll have to see when it happens," I said.

It was on the tip of my lip to talk more about Gail, but I bit down on my tongue and concentrated on my driving instead.

11

Thaddeus Gets Stuck with Two Gilfs

It was quite a chore for tenacious private investigator Thaddeus Black to keep still while seated behind his desk, pretending to appear busy like he had pressing work in front of him. The truth was he had nothing vital on his desk, despite it laden with files and discarded bits of paperwork from ongoing assignments or once he'd recently concluded. Thaddeus seldom minded a clean desk—he left that for his secretary to handle whenever he was out of the office or whenever he closed earlier than she did. If not, then whatever remained on his desk would wait till morning or whenever he felt like being tidy.

Today wasn't one of such days. He had dismissed his secretary hours ago as he had no reason to keep her around; she won't return till Monday. He wanted the remainder of the afternoon for himself since he was expecting company; instead, he was expecting pussy.

Gilf pussy.

He wanted to make it like he had pressing business in hand besides awaiting her arrival. He shouldn't be doing crazy stuff like this, but he didn't care—in his opinion, it was a guaranteed perk that came with the job. Thaddeus was a horny, randy bastard and considered it nonsensical to trick out bitches in bars and nightclubs. Now and then came an interesting client worthy of his time and taste, in this case, a non-client.

Why not take advantage of the situation when he could?

*****

Thaddeus Black's business card bore his work address, which I followed to a capital T as I drove into the city, heading to Clifford Avenue. Whatever had compelled, Richard to change his mind regarding my relationship with Terrence, I know, couldn't have been some utter miracle. Surely, the P.I. had more involvement, and I couldn't wait to hear what he had to say. I knew it would come with a price, so I opted to look my best before leaving the house. Now, with my best friend tagging along, this was sure to be fun.

"Are we any closer to where we're going?" Sarah asked impatiently. "Gosh, it's going to be a long trip returning home."

"Would you relax? You look like you're getting angsty. Besides, we're almost there."

I came to the junction that was B Street by Clifford Avenue, and even my GPS told me I had arrived at my destination. I found the building with the investigator's address but drove past it to find a vacant parking spot, then turned off my engine.

"We're here," I said. "Let's go."

We left the car and strolled toward the building. We ascended a flight of stairs and came to a glass door that said: THADDEUS BLACK Private Investigator. I knocked and waited. A shadow appeared behind the door and Thaddeus opened it and smiled.

"Nice that you could come, Erica." He stopped when he saw I wasn't alone.

"This is my friend, Sarah. She's aware of everything that's happened to me and figured she'd come along and meet you in person. I hope it's no bother."

"No, no, no bother at all," his smile was disarming as he shook Sarah's hand before inviting us into his office.

"Excuse the mess," he said after shutting his door and offered us chairs while he settled on the edge of his desk. "I've been busy with other things. How have things been with you and Richard lately?"

"It's been good, as far as I can see. He wanted to see me have sex with my lover, Terrence, and I did that for him. But I don't know if you talked him down from getting upset."

"After you and I hooked up that other day, he called me up wanting to know whatever you'd been up to or where you'd been. I told him I had tailed you to a beauty salon, and you had been there for a long time. That calmed his nerves."

"I don't understand," Sarah looked at me. "I thought you said Richard had no issue with you and Terrence?"

"This was before he told me to have Terrence over," I explained. "Or maybe he changed his mind after he learned I made it to the salon instead of spending time with Terrence at his friend's place."

"Right you are," Thaddeus agreed. "He's got me on retainer. Probably wants to keep keeping tabs on you."

"And you'll know what to tell him if he calls you again?"

"Well, now, you're going to have to make me an offer I cannot refuse," Thaddeus smiled, giving me the hint. "I've got a side office down the hall where we can talk better."

"Side office?" Sarah asked.

"You can bring your friend along," Thad gestured at Sarah. "Unless you'd prefer she wait here until we return."

"Sarah is used to what I do," I rose to my feet. "I'm sure she'd love to tag along. Come on, Sarah. Let's see what else our handsome P.I. has for us."

Sarah stood up and Thaddeus ushered us out of his office. He went across the hall to another door similar to his. He pulled a key out of his pocket and unlocked it before ushering us inside.

I had no idea what awaited us until he flipped a light switch, and I saw the large bed taking up space in the room. The room was neat but austere; the walls were duly painted—it was a room meant for one thing only, not for comfort.

Thaddeus opened a wall closet and began unbuttoning his shirt. I dropped my handbag on a lone chair and followed suit. Sarah was initially clueless but quickly realized what was about to happen and decided not to be excluded. Thaddeus waited until I had finished discarding my bra and panties into the closet before taking my hand to lead me to the bed; his cock was pressing to climb out of his pair of briefs. Thaddeus had an exemplary build, nearly similar to my lover, Terrence. The instant I grabbed his cock out of his briefs, I knew I was going to enjoy him.

I knelt before him, holding his prick inches from my face, and rolled my tongue around the tip, tasting pre-cum oozing out of his penis slit before engulfing it with my mouth. I observed Sarah curse her clumsiness while she hurried to remove her jeans and then put them away in the closet. I made room for her when she came to join us on the bed. I released my hold on Thad's prick so Sarah could catch up with the fun.

Sarah and I have equal taste in black men and have nourished our share plenty of times. There had been times when we shared a single lover when there weren't others to play with, so this action wasn't novel to us. We've had plenty of fun in her basement, servicing multiple black men while our husbands watched. Back then, Richard was steadfast about ensuring I remained a black cock-whore for whichever black man came calling. He would hurry home to mind the kids while I would stick around with Sarah. What fun times those had been.

"Just like old times, eh?" Sarah remarked as if she could read my mind.

"You know it, girl," I laughed.

Thaddeus lay on his back while we knelt on either side and took turns sucking his cock. Thad caressed both our tits down to our butts while we moaned to counter our separate arousal. I rummaged my hand between my legs and fingered my cunt, getting my pussy motivated. I knew Sarah was doing likewise. She was such a slut and could turn her sex meter from zero to a hundred instantly. She and Aaron have been married for thirty-plus years and have raised three children, the last of which was Gail, who was about to get married, while her two sons had long married and left the coop. Sharon once confessed she'd had the kids so she could become pregnant by Aaron, which was all he was essential for besides being a loving husband and provider. But if she could do it over again, she would prefer getting knocked up by any of her lovers. I, too, expressed a similar confession to her; it was one such moment that guaranteed a tightness to our bond.

I attacked Thaddeus's gorgeous pair of balls, kissing each inch of flesh around the underside of his thighs while Sarah continued to deep-throat his cock, spitting on his shaft before further glistening it with her mouth. We exchanged later, laughing like horny teenagers would as I made his prick stay rock-hard.

The moment came for us to decide who would enjoy him first.

"You go first, Erica," Sarah suggested. "I'll follow your lead."

I would have preferred Sarah to go first, as she hadn't sampled him before, but since she insisted, I took the reins and mounted Thad first. His cock slipped inside my cunt with ease. I impaled myself down to his pelvis and felt goosebumps unleash across my arms the instant I settled firmly on him. Sarah wasted no time smacking my butt, urging me to ride him. My hips came to life and began kicking and sprinting while Thad groped and fondled my hanging pair of tits. Thaddeus pulled me by my tits to lean closer so he could grasp my butt and lift his legs. I leaned over his shoulder, and he pinned me there and suddenly began jerking his hips. I felt his thighs slap my butt with such rapid fire that it knocked the wind out of me. I was gasping and groaning louder uncontrollably. His cock slipped out of my vagina, allowing me to catch my breath. Sarah grabbed his cock, sucked it clean, and then shoved it back into me.

Thad didn't slow his pace as he kept machine gun-pounding me with gusty energy. It felt like he had been saving up for this moment when he would get to unleash what he couldn't give me the last time we fucked. He squeezed my butt with both hands and held a firm grip, punishing me with his throbbing power. I felt his cock hammering my cunt, carving a path straight to my heart, and I was helpless to the wave of euphoria and lust swirling in my head. I felt myself climaxing and couldn't stop screaming with joy. This was beyond what I expected today, and I was thankful for it.

Thaddeus was gasping heavily against my tits. He slowed his pace, letting me ride him slow and steady while his breathing returned to normalcy. We were both sweating with mine rolling down my neckline and dropping on his face. He didn't appear to mind as he entertained himself with sucking my tits and smacking my butt cheeks.

I rolled off him eventually, gasping like I had concluded a marathon race, as Sarah took my place. Like me, Thaddeus upped his game and got Sarah bouncing hard on his cock. She, too, underwent a wailing frenzy while attempting to keep up with his pace. At some point, she stopped, turned in a complete circle, and rode him in reverse. Sarah spread her legs, lifted herself inches from his pelvis, and wiggled her hips while his cock stayed buried in her cunt. I inched forward and tasted the trail of cum oozing down his shaft. I took solace in the foul fragrance coming off them.

Thaddeus fell to his side and pulled Sarah along. He lifted her leg over his thighs to afford room to slide his cock between her legs. His cock kept slipping out of her, and I was quick to suck it clean before returning it into her cunt.

Later, Thad had me on my elbows and knees and fucked me doggy-style. Sarah held my butt cheeks apart so Thad could thrust deep into my cunt. She then aligned herself beside him, and Thad gave her similar medicine. When his moment arrived, he groaned aloud and gestured at us to position ourselves properly. We knew what was expected of us before he even communicated his wish. We knelt before him, shoulders touching, mouths agape, awaiting his release. Thaddeus gasped and groaned aloud as he squirted his load down our throats. We caught much of his semen and later licked each other's face clean.

The afternoon was barely over.

12

Saying Goodbye to a Gilf

I applied a cleanser liquid to my face from a bottle I often carried in my handbag while filling the bathroom sink with water. I waited nearly a minute before splashing water on my face to wash off the cleaner. My facial texture felt brand new when I finished like I'd acquired a recent tan. I washed off the cleanser residue from the sink's surface and admired my new look in the mirror. The door was shut, but I heard the unmistakable, familiar noise coming from beyond that sounded like my best friend, Sarah, was enjoying another round with Thaddeus Black. It seemed like they waited for me to leave the room before they got started.

I smiled and decided to see how far they were going.

I opened the door and peeked inside the bedroom, and sure enough, they were deep into another round of fucking. Thad lay on his side and held up Sarah's leg while jamming his cock where it needed to be. Sarah lay halfway on the bed on her elbow while her other arm went from grasping her bouncing tits to grabbing Thad's arm like she wanted him to take things easy. Her mouth was shaped in an oval form, while her eyes went from appearing half-closed to flaring wide open; her gasps stuttered along with her breathing.

I returned my facial bottle into my handbag, looked at my phone, and saw we had been here more than an hour—like I didn't know that fucking takes up time—the first round had been good, but the one after had been spectacular; Thaddeus knew how to handle pussy, even Sarah commended his unquenchable stamina after making her cum the second time. I had two missed calls, one from Richard and another from Terrence. Who would have thought I'd have my husband and my lover calling me simultaneously? Although Richard's call had come nearly a half-hour before Terrence.

"What you looking at, Erica?"

The question came from Sarah. She was kneeling on the bed, stroking Thaddeus's cock with both hands while glancing at me. Her face was a glistening mask of sweat, but the glee in her eyes showed she was having excellent fun. The type of fun I had promised when we left her place a while ago.

"It's getting late," I said. "We're gonna have to start hitting the road soon before it gets dark."

"Awwhh, can't we stay for a little while longer? I'll bet our friend Thad here won't mind. Do you, Thad?"

"Aren't you supposed to put your mouth where it ought to be?" He indicated at his cock.

"Oh, yeah, how clumsy of me," Sarah replied before applying her mouth where she should.

I opened the closet containing our clothes and found my pair of underwear. Behind me, Sarah was still going at his cock like she'd only begun blowing him; I could have gone and left her there, and she wouldn't have complained. Sarah knows how to lose herself once she gets into her sexual peak, like a NASCAR racer; once she hits her peak, it is often hard for her to scale down. I, too, am like that sometimes; this was one of the few occasions where I was the one having sense.

I wore my panties and slipped into my bra before joining them.

"Come on, Sarah," I wrestled Thaddeus's cock from her grip. "Richard called me a while back and will likely call again. He will get nosey if he knows I'm with you. You go on, get dressed; I'll take care of this for you."

Sarah grumbled but saw meaning in my words and opted to do as I said. Though there wasn't anything seriously wrong about Richard knowing I was with Sarah. Richard would presume, naturally, as he should, that being with Sarah is as toxic as leaving a Catholic nun in a brothel. His worst fear was Sarah putting me back into the ways I once was, worse than him knowing I've got a lover in town that he's now aware of. However, Richard is clueless about me fucking his private eye that he put on my tail; picture the irony of him knowing I've been sharing his private investigator with Sarah. That would give him plenty to think about.

"You sure you wanna leave so soon?" Thad mused while I rolled my lips around the tip of his prick. "Was thinking we can at it for another hour."

"Don't tell me you've got enough gas in your energy tank to last another hour," I said. "You must be tired already."

"Tired, maybe a little," he smiled. "Older pussy often gets me going, though."

I sucked his cock more before replying, "What about the janitor or whoever you've got that cleans these offices for you?"

"He won't be showing up for another two hours plus. But if you've got an urgent place to be, we can always reschedule another date. Or maybe we can have ourselves a quickie before you leave."

I looked at Sarah who seemed unbothered by us, as she then opened the bathroom door and disappeared inside. I had no idea if she intended to take a bath, and it was tempting knowing I had a few minutes to enjoy Thad one final time before calling it a day. Against all odds, I decided to stick with my urges.

"Alright, one quickie," I stood up and maneuvered to get on top of him. "Just one, and that's it."

"That's the spirit, bitch," he crackled.

Thad held me by my waist as he had done a while back while I slid my panties to the side and shoved his cock inside me.

What was supposed to be a quickie became more than that. I'd figured Sarah would only wash her face and privates, but whatever she was in the bathroom for kept her there long enough for Thaddeus to roll over on the bed, pinning me under his bulk and then pounding me hard. I would have figured he'd be less inclined to go the distance, but possibly mature pussy does keep him going. Sarah returned from the bathroom and joined us, though it was rather late on her part. Thad's discharge was of less quantity than previous, but it was all the better. He saved up enough strength to see us back into our clothes and escort us out of his building.

We waved goodbye to Thad before heading to where I had parked my car. I used the time to call Richard to find out why he had called. It was our daughter, Linda. She wanted to know if I'd be home tomorrow; there was something she wanted to talk to me about. Richard didn't know what it was but figured it wasn't anything serious. He didn't ask where I was, and I didn't tell him. That would wait until I get home, and only if he inquired.

The sky was purple and the sun was a golden orange ball, hanging low on the horizon when Sarah and I drove home. She was in a cheerful spirit, the same as me. I felt completely different, and re-energized, unlike when I left home for Sarah's place. Looking at Sarah, I saw the same qualities I was experiencing. We looked like we had embarked on an expensive carnival ride and still basking in the adventure. What made it special was that our husbands weren't involved in what we had done today; this was a secret, like so many other secrets we have shared, and we intend to keep it to ourselves for now.

But then my mind started keeping up with other signals, and one happened to be the conversation I had with Sarah's daughter, Gail, before leaving her home. That would have to keep until the next time Gail and I had a chance to sit and talk.

I dropped Sarah off and promised to keep in touch with her later before heading home. Richard was sitting on the veranda reading a newspaper when I pulled into the driveway. He gave me a curious look as I came over and kissed his cheek, and it got me worried as I feared there was something on me that I hadn't noticed throughout my drive from the city.

"What's with the happy look on your face?" Richard asked.

"What are you talking about?"

"You're looking way too happy than when you left, is what. You went over to see your friend, Terrence?"

"No, I didn't go to see Terrence, and I'm not lying, so don't give me that nasty look like you think I'm lying."

"I wasn't thinking anything, darling. If you say you didn't go to see him, then I believe you. In fact, this is one recent time when I believe you more than ever."

"Whatever makes you think that?"

He waved his hand dismissively. "Don't worry about it; you'll find out soon enough. You think you can scrounge us some dinner?"

"Yeah, sure. Let me go inside."

I entered the house and made for the kitchen. Something compelled me to stop, and then I remembered Terrence's phone call and wondered whatever he had called me about and why he never bothered texting me. I went upstairs to the bedroom, dropped my handbag on the bed then sat down and dialed his number.

"What's up, babe?" Terrence spoke into my ear.

"Hi. I got your missed call. Sorry, I couldn't answer at the time."

"It's not a big deal. Good thing you called now, or you won't hear from me for another two hours, maybe not till tomorrow."

"What are you talking about, babe?"

"I'm at the airport right now, jetting off to see some family in Florida."

"Oh. I didn't know…I thought I was going to come and see you tomorrow."

"Sorry, babe. It was a sudden thing, and I needed to step in. I left some stuff with Ken to give to you, though you're going to have to call him about it. I'll text you his number before I leave."

"Okay. How long are you going to be gone?"

"About a week," said Terrence. "Maybe more. But we'll see how things go. I'll talk to you later, babe. Bye."

I barely had time to reply before the line ended. Suddenly, my happy feeling for the day was leaving me empty.

13

Heartbreak and Revelations
for a Gilf

That night I struggled with sleep. My heart was torn in half, one part with discontent and the other with nothing but pity; pity toward myself. I lay on my side of the bed recalling my conversation with Terrence. My source of discontent was with the tone of his voice and how abruptly he ended the call like he couldn't bear to speak with me anymore. Was this the end of my relationship with him, or was I jumping to conclusions?

I clutched my pillow under my head as I lay on my side. My knees were clasped together under the covers. Behind me echoed light snoring coming from Richard. How would he respond if I told him that Terrence was traveling, leaving me alone with nobody to play with? With nobody to have fun with when next do I decide to go swimming at the YMCA?

Is there nobody? Really?

Well, not really. There is the shrewd P.I. Thaddeus Black, but he isn't my lover (or maybe he is, and I'm looking at things differently). He isn't Terrence, even though he sure is polite to talk to and incredible to fuck, too. Maybe I could see about frequenting with him, anything to make up for whenever Terrence returns from Florida. I called his number hours after Richard and I ate dinner but got nothing; I left him a voicemail message to call me later. Hopefully, he'll respond once he arrives at where he was going.

I tried not to read anything deceptive into our conversation, but then I recalled Richard's snarky remark when I returned home. It sounded so foreboding what he had said. I didn't want to assume he was aware of this, and if so, what could I possibly do about it? I checked the time on my phone and saw it was 01:13 a.m. I shut my eyes and forced myself into sleep.

Morning arrived, and nothing about the world changed when I awoke. That was unfortunate because I felt wearier from the little sleep I got. There was a throbbing in my forehead that felt like the onset of a nasty headache. I swallowed an aspirin pill and later felt better.

Linda arrived hours later without the kids. It had been a while since that happened, though she looked cheerful and sunny when she kissed my cheek. Richard asked about Jeffery, her husband. I observed my daughter's face as she said Jeffery was great and out to work even before she woke up. Jeffery worked as a technical engineer and was often too busy to visit except for a few occasions when Linda succeeded to drag him over. She explained that she had driven the kids to a daycare camp before making her way over. I made some fruit brunch and offered some to Richard, who took his plate to the den to watch a game. I led Linda out back to the patio where we could be alone and out of earshot. My dog, Polly, followed and lay beside my feet while Linda sat beside me.

"Richard said you sounded worried when you called yesterday," I said.

"Dad worries too much when he shouldn't."

"Maybe he does. But is everything all right, dear?"

"As far as I can tell," she swept her hair from her face but focused her gaze on something in front of her instead. Her voice sounded uncertain as she spoke. "Everything's great, but…there's something that's been going on. Something I figured I'd best talk to you about."

"Anything to do with Jeffery?"

"Yeah, it does." She fell silent, then adjusted herself in her chair to face me. "I've got something to tell you, Mom. Promise you won't tell Dad or anybody."

"Your secret is my secret, honey. What is it?"

"I've been cheating on Jeffery," Linda blurted but stopped to catch herself; too late. She took a moment to compose herself while I, too, tried to rearrange my mind regarding what my daughter was about to spill.

"I'm sorry, Mom. That came out the wrong way; I apologize."

"Tell me what's been going on, dear," I applied my best motherly tone that's known to calm whatever situation in the room. "You've been cheating on Jeffery."

"Yes, I've been a bad girl. I've been cheating on him, and I can't stop."

"What do you mean? First, who's the fellow you're spending time with?"

"It is not just one fellow, Mom," she explained. "It's several. I've been sleeping with three different men for the past several months. I shouldn't be doing it, but I can't make myself stop; I almost don't want to stop seeing them."

"Almost?"

"Sorry, I mean I do want to—maybe that's the wrong word I'm using—but I feel stopping will take away something from me. Something I'm afraid of losing."

My expression didn't change, but I was inwardly wrestling with my daughter's profound situation and trying not to seem more confused than I was.

"Who are these men you're sleeping with? Are they connected?"

"Two things connect them. One is they're both black," Linda revealed. "The second is they're Jeffery's friends; they were part of his groom train at our wedding."

"But you said Jeffery has no idea."

"Not exactly," she explained. "Jeffery does know, partly. The whole thing was his idea in the first place."

It felt like déjà vu listening to my daughter narrate the clandestine lifestyle she and her husband had been living for months. I would have loved to hurry her along to the point where she started experiencing her conscience crisis. I worried that the longer we sat on the patio would attract Richard to speculate about our discussion. But I didn't want to throw Linda off her groove, not when she was going through a similar lifestyle as mine. This was a unique occurrence, and I was double-mind how to react.

"Jeffery and I do have sex," Linda began. "But it's usually a sporadic sort—sometimes we'd go weeks before we approached making love. It's been like this since, way before we got married. I once thought it was a passing phase. I figured things would change after we took our vow. Then I began noticing stuff about him that seemed weird. Jeffery masturbates a lot. He does it discreetly when I'm not aware: in the bathroom when he's taking a bath and elsewhere around the house. I kept seeing dry semen stains in his briefs and on the towels. Besides that, he often sneaks out of bed late at night to watch porn. I didn't mind at first— I pretended not to notice sometimes—but then it got too much, so I confronted him. This was weeks before our wedding. He confessed about his nasty habit of watching interracial porn and how he fancies seeing me as one of the women screwing black men in the porn videos he watched."

"Really, he admitted to that?"

"He did," Linda said, then continued. "We had a long talk about it. We talked about seeing a therapist if things grew worse. I feared he was addicted and couldn't decide how to deal with it. I wanted to help Jeffery however I could. He said the best way to help was if I had sex with one of his buddies, Rick."

"And you did," I answered the question for her.

"I did. I figured it would do fine to make Jeffery happy—I was going to marry him no matter what—it wouldn't look good if we ended like this. Also, I was kinda curious about Rick. I mean, I do kind of fancy him, but not that I was ever thinking of screwing someone besides Jeffery. We had talked about Rick before. One time, when we got drunk, he asked if I ever had the nerve to cheat, who would I do it with? Silly me, I mentioned Rick. He brought up that episode, and that was how he talked me into doing it. He said he wanted to see what connection we might have, and if I don't like it, then I can call it quits, and he won't ever bring it up again. He said he would talk it over with Rick, and days later, he told me Rick agreed. We checked into a hotel, and that was when it happened."

"What happened, dear?" I prodded her like I didn't know already what happened. I was no fool, but inside, I was salivating to hear what my daughter had to say about her infidelity. Her words boosted my morale, but I struggled not to let any of it spill out of my face.

Linda shrugged before continuing her tale. "Jeffery and I waited, and minutes later, Rick showed up. Jeffery didn't want me feeling nervous, so he decided to leave us alone. Things started out awkward, but then Rick kissed me. I kissed him back, and the next thing, I had my arms around him while he locked me around his. We fell on the bed and then…well, we spent a while making out—foreplay, I mean—it was kinda like making love, which was something I'd missed from Jeffery—then we got out of our clothes. I looked at Rick's cock, and knew I wanted him bad."

"How was it like with him? Making love to Rick, I mean."

"It was sex, Mom, not lovemaking," Linda laughed while she corrected me. "That's how I'd like to see it. But yeah, the sex was good; way better than I expected and anything Jeffery and I had done. The sex got me hooked, Mom. I swear, after that night, I couldn't stop thinking about Rick and his cock, and of when I would have a chance of fucking him again." Linda stopped abruptly when she said that. "I'm sorry, Mom. I didn't mean to get carried away like that."

"You couldn't help it, dear," I muttered. Seriously, I loved that she had uttered that word to me and would have told her to say it more often as she continued about her second and third encounters with Rick.

"The second time happened at the hotel again—this was a week later—this time, Jeffery decided to stay and watch; I felt confident about myself and didn't mind, and neither did Rick—"

"You let him use a condom, right?" I interrupted. "And where were the kids while this was happening?"

Linda blushed when she spoke. "Yes, he did use a condom. But that went away the third time, and that happened at our place—doing it at the hotel didn't seem comfortable enough. Rick was fuc—I mean, we were deep into the sex when suddenly he stopped and pulled out. I found out his condom had popped. But I wanted him so damn bad. I ripped the torn condom off his—you-know-what—and let him raw-dog me. Jeffery was shocked by what I did, but he didn't stop us; I wouldn't have allowed him. Rick seemed enthused by my bold gesture. He lay on top of me and kept giving it to me, harder and harder. As for the kids, Jeffery had taken them to spend the weekend with his parents in Chicago."

"I see. But Rick didn't cum inside you?" I was eager to hear the juicy part.

"He pulled out in time and came all over me. And then Jeffery did the most astonishing thing I could ever imagine, Mom. He came over and licked every trace of Rick's semen off my body and torso. Finished, he then mounted me, and we had the most amazing sex ever!"

I would have fallen off my chair when she said those last words if I weren't already leaning forward while grabbing the armrests. I did feel shock, but it was a shock mixed with joy and unexpected happiness.

I excused myself and told Linda I would return in a minute; I indicated that Polly stay put while I entered the house. I stood against the kitchen counter to catch my breath, then went to see about Richard. He wasn't alone in the den; his golfing buddy, Avery, who lived a block from us, was enjoying the game with him. I turned away from their laughter and went to a nearby restroom to check my temperature. I splashed water on my face and wished I had time to remain there to masturbate. Instead, I dried my face and returned to Linda, still seated at the patio.

"My God, Linda," I gasped as I returned to my chair, flustered and amazed by everything she had said so far but also by the swirling emotion her words were unleashing inside me. I felt a throbbing electricity coursing along my veins, wishing I had someone to share it with, someone like Terrence. "There's more to this, right?"

"I haven't gotten to the part where I started screwing Jeffery's other friends," she said.

I checked my watch. It felt like the day was going to get longer.

14

More Revelations for a Gilf

An hour had passed since Linda began narrating her story to me. Had it been anyone else, I would have called a time-out and declared that we continue some other day. Except this was my daughter, and the stuff she had revealed to me wasn't to be taken lightly. I was clueless, however, if she'd seriously come to me for advice or to share her intimate sexual activities. What would her husband, Jeffery, think if he found out we had been discussing such?

I returned to the house to check on Richard if he and his friend needed anything. They were still deep into the game; the table was laden with beers and snacks, so they didn't require my presence.

"You haven't said anything about the other two," I reminded Linda. She had followed me upstairs to the bedroom, which I figured was safer than the patio. Richard won't come looking for me without me knowing. I folded some clothes and put them away in my closet while Linda played with Polly's fur.

"I was going to get to that, Mom. Jeffery knows nothing about them, which made me come to talk to you about it."

"Go ahead then," I finished putting clothes away in the closet and then came to sit beside her. "I'm all ears."

"Jeffery hasn't any problem with Rick and I having sex," she explained. "Rick and I have had sex often without Jeffery around, though I usually tell him afterward. I was over at Rick's place one day—he had called his office to say he had a fever and couldn't make it, but it was so we could have enough fun together—Jeffery knew about this and didn't mind. We'd finished having sex, and then we talked about including others. I don't know why, but I was so warmed up by the thought of sleeping with more men. It didn't help that Rick and I were smoking weed—Oops, sorry, Mom. I didn't mean for you to know that."

"With everything you've told me so far, you're going to stop on that?" We both chuckled at my expense. "I know what weed does, and your dad does take it now and then. But that's for another day, continue."

"Yeah, so, Rick and I had been puffing on grass and I was probably half-stoned out of my mind. I was stoned, I was horny, so it kinda made for a perfect moment to say yes to whatever he suggested. He reached for his phone, called up two of his friends, and told them to come around. They showed up later, and the three of them had their way with me."

"Just to be clear, they didn't rape you, did they?"

"No, of course not, Mom. I can't go into details, you understand, but knew what they were doing to me, and I enjoyed it."

"Okay, I just wanted to be clear on that. And you never mentioned that part to Jeffery?"

"That's the problem, Mom. I don't know whether to tell him or keep it as my secret. Rick hasn't mentioned it to him—he'd have told me if he had. Plus, I know Jeffery would have mentioned it already unless he knows but pretends not to, but I doubt it. So, what do you think I ought to do, Mom?"

"I've got another question to ask, dear. Are you worried that if Jeffery finds out, and let's say he doesn't agree, he will cut you off from being with Rick, or tell you to end things with those other guys? What is it that you're most worried about?"

Linda looked away for a moment, lost in thought. I could almost feel sympathy for her regarding what she was grappling with. The similarities to mine are there. Richard never would have agreed if I'd mentioned Terrence to him in the first place, as he equally displayed when he found out. Maybe things would have been different had it been years back when he hadn't gotten advanced with his ailment. The same should befall Linda, I figured, unless she had reasons not wanting to let her husband be part of the fun she was having.

"I guess…I'd love to tell him, and I'm angry with myself for not doing that already…I guess I'm afraid it might hurt Jeffery if he ever finds out I've been fooling around behind his back."

"That's something you'll have to get over, dear. As long as you love each other, I think he will go easy on things. Or, if you want to be certain, then be subtle about it. Don't tell him everything directly. Next time you're making out, broach the subject. Find out what he'd think about you having extra lovers."

"Yeah, I never thought of that before. Maybe I'll give that a try. Thanks, Mom."

"It's what I'm here for, dear. And like I said, your secret is mine as well."

A day later.

"Your secret is mine as well," Sarah muttered, then turned to me. "That was what you told Linda?"

"Yes, it is. What else would you have wanted me to say?"

"I don't know. Maybe tell her about what you and Richard did when you were about her age," said Linda. "Or you can tell her about what you've been doing lately. I'm surprised Linda's never known anything about that part of your life; not even your other kids."

"I guess Richard and I were way too careful not to let them know," I mused. "That part's never easy when you've got a houseful of kids."

We sat by the pool's edge at the YMCA, beating our legs back and forth in the warm, intoxicating water of the swimming pool, while around us, other women, the majority of them about the same age range as us, prattled about while floating in the pool. Sarah and I pretended to be removed from the fray while I told her my conversation with Linda yesterday.

I didn't tell her that I still hadn't heard from Terrence. Not once did my phone ring and it was him. Like the previous night, last night hadn't been easy for me. I kept rolling on my side; sometimes, I even stirred Richard, though he never came awake. At some point, I woke up past midnight and went downstairs to get a glass of water for my parched throat. I felt like I was coming down with a fever, though it was more of a projection. I thought of calling Terrence to find out if anything was the matter—had he gotten in some trouble or what? I feared that making the call might wake Richard; I couldn't help thinking he had something to do with whatever was going on with Terrence.

"Are you listening to me, Erica?"

Sarah bumped her shoulder against mine, which pulled me out of my thoughts.

"Uh? I'm sorry, what was it you said?"

"Looks like you were miles away from here. Are you okay?"

"Yeah, sure, I'm fine. What was it you said?"

"I wanted to know when you want to go see that handsome investigator guy, the one we spent time with the other day; I forget his name."

"Thaddeus Black. I don't know unless I call to know how busy he is; what do you have in mind?"

"What do you think, girl?" Sarah grinned. "I was feeling naughty when I woke up this morning before you called and asked if I'd want to come swimming with you. Maybe we can get together with him again soon, or what do you think?"

We got back into the pool, swarmed several laps before deciding we'd had enough, and went to wash up in the dressing room.

"I thought you have plenty around taking good care of you," I said while we sat on the bench, putting on lotion and wearing back our clothes. Other women entered the room, and I waved and said hello to several before continuing my action.

"Not everything has been going well for me like they've been for you, Erica." Sarah glanced around, making sure we were alone, before continuing in a low voice. "I haven't been getting much luck lately. Most of my former lovers haven't been corresponding back—maybe it's because I'm getting old, so obviously, it's natural to let an old dog die on her own. I haven't had incredible sex like the one we had the other day. I miss that feeling. Why else do you think I envy what you have with Terrence? He's been good to you."

"Yeah, he sure has been," I replied, trying not to show my disappointment.

"How is he doing anyway?"

"He's doing good. He left for Florida to see about some family stuff."

We finished dressing, picked our bags into which we had stuffed our outfits, towels, and other items, and then left the room. I was unprepared for the sun's glare when I pushed past the glass doors and stepped into the YMCA courtyard. Even Sarah gasped and fished out her sunglasses from her handbag as we strolled toward the parking grounds. She had come with her car, and it was parked beside mine.

"I can tell you're missing Terrence."

"Terribly," I said. "I wish he was around. I've got some things I need to pick up before heading home."

"All right, catch you later."

We said our goodbyes and then drove our separate ways. I dialed a number on my phone to let the person at the other end know I was on my way.

I wore my shades and switched to my favorite radio channel, blasting country-rock music while driving. My mind wasn't at peace, but the music was helping; it felt like a tranquil antidote for whatever I was expecting where I was heading. The good thing was he would be home before I arrived; whatever it was wouldn't take long.

The drive took me twenty-plus minutes to get there. I couldn't tell which was his car as I eased into the parking space and switched off my engine. I called to be sure he was home; he responded that he was and for me to come up. I exited my car, took off my sunglasses, and strolled into the apartment building. Minutes later, I stopped in front of his door and pressed the doorbell. The door opened, and it was Ken. His shirt was open with his tie undone.

"Hi, Erica," he smiled. "Glad you came by."

"Hi, Ken. Terrence told me you had some things he wanted to give to me."

"Sure. Come in."

He opened the door for me to enter, which I did, and then shut it behind me.

15

What's Love to a Gilf?

I turned to face Ken as he shut the door and asked, "What's going on here, Ken? What sort of game are you and Terrence playing?"

"Has Terrence called you lately?"

"No. He told me there was something he wanted me to come and get from you, which is why I'm here. But I don't like this merry-go-round type of game that's going on. I need to know what's happened if anything has happened."

"Some things have happened, Erica. But it ain't your fault, and you might find that hard to believe."

He gestured at me to sit down, which I did, taking my handbag off my shoulder and propping it on my thigh.

"I'm owed an explanation, Ken. I haven't spoken to Terrence for two days—I haven't called him, and he hasn't called me."

"Have you been over to his apartment?"

"No, I haven't. Why?"

"I'm going to tell you a bit of what Terrence told me," Ken said. "But the other bit is stuff I pieced together myself. Terrence isn't coming back."

"What?" I felt like someone had punched my face.

"That's what he told me to tell you, but not implicitly. My guess is he's too ashamed to tell you himself. He's locked up his apartment; a moving company is supposed to arrive today to begin packing his stuff. It's so sudden; he's already squared things with his landlord to get compensated for the remaining months before his ten expires."

"My God. Why?"

"He told me he found some better opportunity in Florida and chose to take it. But that's what he told me, I swear."

I reclined my elbows on my knees and ran my fingers through my hair. My worst dreams were suddenly a reality. I shouldn't have been surprised, yet I was, and hurt, too. This was something I'd feared wasn't true, except it was. I felt devastated and hurt.

"But why couldn't...why couldn't I just tell me?" I pleaded.

"I don't know. But if you ask me, his going away thing seemed too sudden. That's my bit."

I fished out my phone and called Terrence, but only got his voicemail. That added further pain to my frustration.

"Why is he being so cowardly and not wanting to answer the phone?"

Ken shrugged as if to say I should have figured this part out already.

"Well, I guess the cookie has crumbled," I remarked and got up. "Looks like there's nothing worth doing about it. Thanks for everything, Ken."

He walked me to his door but stopped me as I was about to leave.

"I'm gonna feel like an asshole saying this, Erica, but if maybe you still need a good time—if you get horny or otherwise—give me a call. My door's always open."

My mind was still in a cluster, and I couldn't decide what to say; instead, I nodded and walked away. My feet seemed to drag as I exited the building, got into my car, and then drove off.

I stopped at a red light traffic and was looking ahead, but my thoughts were elsewhere. I didn't know when the light turned green until vehicles irritably blew their horn at me, and then I quickly got into gear and turned right. It occurred to me that I had taken the wrong route to head home. But after noting that thought, it was followed by another more pleasant than returning home to simmer in my heartache. I switched gears and drove steadily, not bothering to make a call to announce my impending visit.

I knocked on his door and waited. A woman's voice informed me to enter, and I did. A blonde woman occupied a corner table working on a computer with a lit cigarette dangling from her lip. I assumed her to be his secretary, except she looked too classy to be one unless I was mistaken.

"Hi," the blonde woman smiled, extracting the cigarette and blowing smoke above her head. "May I help you?"

"I'd like to see Thaddeus Black, please."

"Have you got an appointment?"

"Not really, no, but he's aware of me; you can tell him it's Mrs. Erica Tennyson."

The blonde stood up, placed her cigarette on an ashtray, and approached Thaddeus' office door. She knocked before entering and was back seconds later, smiling wilder than previous.

"Mr. Black will see you," she opened the door for me. I thanked her and went inside.

Thaddeus rose from behind his desk to welcome me. He wore a white shirt with suspenders and a tie. He exuded an aura of raw masculinity as he approached—the perfect antidote to what I was feeling.

"You're looking good today, Erica," he kissed my cheek, then stepped back to appraise me better. "Sexy and gorgeous for a Tuesday," he added.

"You might say that, except I don't feel like it," I replied. "I'm sorry I didn't call to let you know I was coming; it was a spur of the moment thing."

"You're here, and that's what matters," he led me to a chair and propped himself on his desk. "You're looking gloomy today. Everything good?"

"I wish I could say. That's a pretty secretary you've got there," I indicated at his door.

"Sarah's been with me a long while now. She's helped me in more ways than I can commend her. But she's feisty when she wants to be."

"How feisty are we talking about?"

"She's highly resourceful like any secretary should be, but she's got a craving for sex. She loves to fuck, and goes crazy whenever I bust a nut."

I couldn't stop myself from laughing; that helped to uncoil my tension. "My God, isn't there a woman you won't want to stick your dick into?"

"I can't help it if a woman loves bad boys with a huge cock, can I? Like with you, you look like you can use some good dick right now."

"Really? Can you tell just from looking at me?"

"Besides looking at you, I can smell it on you. You look like you had a bad day; nothing cures bad days than a good fuck."

"Yeah, you're probably right. How about that back room of yours from last time? Is it still available?"

"Let's go find out."

Thad took my hand and led me out of his office.

"Look after things for me, Sarah," he told his secretary. "I'll be back in a bit."

I glanced at Sarah and caught a peculiar smile on her face as he opened his door and ushered me outside; she knew damn well what was up.

Thad ushered me to the same back room as last time. Nothing about the room had changed except for the sheets.

"I wonder who else you've brought here since I was here," I remarked as I dropped my handbag on a chair and started removing my clothes.

"Would it surprise you if I said that ain't nobody been here since?" Thad answered as he, too, was busy taking off his suspenders. "But I won't expect you to believe me."

"The answer I wanted to hear was whether that matters," I said.

"Damn right, it don't." He unbuttoned his shirt and then came at me. "You're here, and that's what fucking matters."

I wrapped my arms over his shoulders as we kissed. My jeans hung loosely around my waist; Thaddeus slipped his hands under my backside to grab a handful of my butt. He helped me out of my remaining clothes, and then I lay on the bed waiting for him to rid himself of his; his cock stood cocksure and ready. He came onto the bed, and I handled his pipe with my mouth while he reached over and caressed my pussy underneath my panties. I moaned while he slipped his fingers beyond my vulva, stirring my sexual imagination. Thoughts of Terrence slipped from my mind the longer I sucked his cock, attacking it with eager pleasure. I rolled his testicles in my mouth and lay on my back while he straddled my face. Thad slipped my panties down my thighs, and I wiggled them off my legs so he could 69 me. He wrapped his arms under my butt and fingered my scrotum while lapping his tongue on my clitoris. My excitement surpassed my feverish mark. It wasn't enough for me to suck his cock anymore—I wanted him inside my cunt terribly.

Thaddeus came off my face, and I adjusted myself on the bed, ready for him to bring that black dick home. Thad knelt between my thighs and rubbed his prick's head against my clit, stirring my horniness further as I helplessly squirmed.

"You're going to give me that dick now, or do you want me waiting till November?"

"Funny, I thought November's still far down the road," he quipped.

"Give me that black dick, you fucking fool," I groaned impatiently.

He edged closer and gave it to me, and it was beautiful.

Thad jerked his cock inside me. Each stroke seemed to open my cunt wide, compelling me to absorb more pleasure than I could handle; I could almost feel his prick easing past my cervix, tunneling its way toward my heart. The feeling was intensely pleasurable, and I wanted more—I craved more. I caressed Thad's arms up to his torso, which seemed to expand as he thrust inside me. His face grew darker and more enhanced each time he exhaled. He fell on me, and I wrapped my arms and feet over him, enshrining him like a cocoon of love.

"This is what I've been wanting all day," I murmured as I caressed the back of his neck and back to his shoulders.

Thad lifted his face, and we kissed passionately while our bodies steadily grounded against each other. I inhaled his breath as he did mine; it felt like a grounded union.

There was a light tap on the door, and it eased open to reveal his secretary. Sarah slipped into the room, shut the door, and then stood there observing us. I looked at her past Thad's shoulders; she looked at me and waved shyly before coming to occupy the chair. She lifted her skirt and inserted her hand into her panties while Thaddeus continued to jerk into me harder and harder. My moans grew flippantly wild. Thad returned to his kneeling position, propped my feet over his shoulders, and grunted while slamming into me. Each thrust felt like a gloved fist rammed into my gut—it hurt like it was supposed to, but in its wake was a quelling sense of pleasure.

Sarah left the chair and came to Thaddeus's side. Thad turned to her, and they kissed lengthy while he maintained his pace.

"I figured you'd want some dick too," Thad told his secretary.

"You know me well, boss," she said. "Why let everyone else have all the fun except me?"

Thad pulled out and got me to turn around. At the same time he was fucking me from behind, Sarah was discarding her clothes, leaving each item on the floor beside mine. She came onto the other side of the bed and squeezed my tits while Thaddeus kept fucking me hard; he gripped my waist and forced me backward to hammer home his cock. I lowered my face onto the bed and gripped the sheets, groaning from the mounting pleasure and pain. I overheard Sarah urging me to take that dick…keep taking it…and somewhere amid my delirium, I muttered that I was taking it…*I was taking the dick!*

Thaddeus let me go, and then Sarah assumed my former position. I lay on my back and watched them while massaging my pussy, feeling smoke curl out from the bout of fucking I had just endured. Sarah smiled at me, but her smile became a rictus of pain and lust as she began suffering the brute pounding from her boss.

Thaddeus oozed sweat and manliness out of his pores. He gritted his teeth, and his face curled into a mask of strength as he further distilled his power. He upped his pace and fucked his secretary harder. I came and lay beside Sarah, allowing her to suck on my tits while she moaned aloud her lust. Thad pulled out of her and hurriedly returned to me. He fucked me hard and fast this time; I luxuriated in the feel of his balls slapping my butt faster.

I could feel his prick expanding in my cunt and knew he was seconds from reaching his moment.

"Come inside me, babe," I moaned while squeezing my eyes shut from the onslaught of his cock. "Ohhh fucking give it to me, babe!"

Thaddeus tensed against me, and seconds later, I, too, tensed and lifted my feet above his elbows as he ejaculated inside me. I screamed from the sudden rush and could barely clench my toes are more cum flooded my cunt. Sarah waited for Thad to retrieve his prick before sticking her face between my legs as I gradually returned to earth from the clouds.

I felt like a completely different woman by the time I left Thaddeus for home, smiling proudly behind my sunglasses.

16

From a Gilf to a Snowbunny
Pt. 1

"I had a fun time yesterday."

"How good of a fun time are we talking about here," Sarah inquired. A moment's pause, then she declared, "You went and got fucked, didn't you, you dirty, horny-ass bitch!"

I laughed, but not loud enough to stir my grandson, Brandon, sleeping on the cot bed I had made for him in the living room. Brandon belonged to my son, whose wife came by and dropped him off before taking off. She and my son had hectic work schedules that barely afforded them time to find a nanny to care for their son. Of course, why waste money hiring a nanny when you've got a Granny like me around? It was the least I could do since I had much time on my hands than sitting at home watching re-runs of NCIS or Law & Order series day after day, especially when Richard left me to my own devices while he tended to his.

The TV was on, and Barney, the jolly purple dinosaur, was singing a medley with a group of kids, but the volume was on mute so that I could answer Sarah while trying my best not to wake my grandson.

"Who was it, Erica? Was it that same P.I. guy we enjoyed last time?"

"Thaddeus Black, yes, it was him. But it wasn't pre-planned. I was feeling lost with myself when I left the YMCA. I had some errands to take care of, and I wasn't even thinking when I cruised by his office."

"Yeah, yeah, yeah. You went cruising by because you needed some of that big black cock to yourself. But I'm not upset; the main thing is you had fun. How was it this time? Was it as great as when we tag-teamed on him?"

"It sure was," I smiled inwardly. I knew Sarah was peeved about me having fun alone, but wasn't too hurt since it was me. Nothing else gets her reeled besides missing out on some good sex; I would have to make it up to her later. I left where I was sitting and approached a window, looking out into my front yard. "Like last time, we weren't alone together."

"What do you mean?"

"He's got this pretty-looking secretary who wanted in on the action—no, she wasn't there when we went by—she was fun to play with, too. But I knew you'd be upset—"

"No, I'm not upset, Erica. Well, maybe a little," Sarah chuckled.

"Who's to say you shouldn't be? But don't wor—"

Words froze in my mouth when I saw a car stop in front of the house. The door opened, and a woman came out of the driver's side; it was Sarah's daughter, Gail. Instantly, I thought my eyes were playing tricks on me. I almost didn't want to believe it was her until she left her vehicle and strolled into my driveway, approaching my house. I parted the curtains further, and Gail saw me and waved; that made everything real.

"Sarah, it looks like my grandson just woke up," I told my friend. "I'm going to have to call you later."

"Okay, sure. Talk later, Erica. Bye."

I said goodbye to her and ended the call right before my doorbell rang. I opened it and there stood Gail on my porch, smiling.

"Good afternoon, Aunt Erica," said Gail before hugging me; she was blushing even as she spoke, resembling every bit like the shy, diffident girl I've always known her to be since she was little. Hard to imagine she was weeks away from getting married. Then it won't be long before she got pregnant and started farming her own litter of children.

"I'm sorry if my visit is rather impromptu."

"Think nothing of it, Gail. How's your mom doing?"

"She's doing great; I was with her this morning."

I invited her inside but indicated to be quiet as I went to check on my grandson, who was still asleep and not even stirring. I invited Gail to join me in the kitchen.

"I was going to make myself some coffee. You care for some?"

"No, Aunt, I'm good. I'm sorry I didn't call earlier to let you know I was coming."

"It's no big deal," I fixed some espresso with the coffee machine. "You kind of caught me off guard with the stuff you mentioned the other day," I said as I approached the table. I held my cup to my face and blew into my coffee while gathering my thoughts. "What was it that you wanted to know about?"

Gail gave me an earnest look and asked, "I want to know what it's like to have sex with a black man. I can't ask my mom for obvious reasons, but figure you're the best person to inquire about it."

"Why would you ever want to inquire about it?"

"I dunno, I'm a bit nosy, I guess."

"That's not enough of an answer, Gail. You're on your way to getting married; why throw that away for this?"

"I'm not throwing anything away, Aunt. I'm still going to get married to Jeffery, no matter what. I just want to know whatever fun that's out there that I'm missing out on."

"Fun?" I chuckled before taking a sip of my espresso. "You've got your life ahead of you. What could possibly have gotten you to want to know about this?"

"Because it's something my friends have done that I haven't," Gail pouted. "I was with my friends the day before I spoke with you, and they told me about how big—that was the way they put it—black men tend to be. One of my friends, Carol, showed me a nude photo of her boyfriend— he's black—and he looked big, way bigger than any I've seen." Gail gave a girlish laugh. "I asked her how come she was able to take him on. She said he usually hurts her, but she can't help enjoying it."

"Ahhh. And that's what got you to come to me?"

"To tell the truth, I've been wanting to talk to you about this for a while now. I didn't know how to present it, and I worried my mom would hear. I'd like this talk we're having to remain between us."

"Your secret is my secret, Gail. I promise I won't utter a word to your mom. But if you truly want an answer to this, then you're going to have to find out the hard way. Do you get what I mean?"

"I'm going to have to sleep with a black man?"

"Not sleep, honey. Fuck; there's a big difference." I drained my espresso before continuing. "You're going to get married soon, so it's obvious you and your future husband have already started having sex, right?"

Gail nodded.

"Having sex with a black man might seem like a no-big-deal thing, but trust me, it's unlike anything you can ever experience, Gail. It's nothing compared to you being with your fiancé or me with my husband. There is the sex, but the sex is greater than anything you've ever had before. And it's way more addictive than a cup of coffee or a cigarette. Are you sure you want to learn more about this?"

"Yes," Gail said without hesitation. "Yes, Aunt, I do. You don't think I'm crazy for wanting this, do you?"

"When I was about your age, I probably asked myself the same question. I don't recall if I ever found the answer I wanted. But I was glad I had Richard—I would have been lost in this journey without him. He and I were tight about what we wanted."

"That's the same way I feel about my mom and dad. I get upset with myself sometimes knowing the stuff I've found out lately, but not back then. I've sneaked into their basement room and even found some old tapes they did of Mom having sex with other men—pretty wild the stuff they were into—I even watched ones that had you and Uncle Richard in them."

"You've kept this to yourself, I trust?"

"Your secret is my secret, Aunt Erica," she said. "Why would I go about telling anyone such crazy stuff?"

"I'm glad you didn't. I've got a friend who I can introduce you to, who would make better acquaintance with you. I'll give him a call to find out when he's going to be free, but that's if you're interested in going further about this."

"I am, Aunt Erica. Please, whatever you can."

"I'll do what I can, all right. Whether you end up liking the end result is going to be up to you. I'd better go check on my grandkid."

Later that night, I sat up reading a novel when Richard exited the bathroom and slipped into bed. My book lay open before my legs, holding my concentration.

"How was your day?"

"It was good," I answered. "How was yours?"

"Shot a birdie out on the eighth hole today. You're not feeling sleepy yet?"

"I will in a while. I've got this page to finish, and then I'm done."

He laid his head on his pillow and was silent for a moment.

"How's Terrence doing?"

"I really wouldn't know, hon."

"You ain't called him since?"

"Why bother? He will whenever he wants."

"That's a shame," Richard remarked. "I guess you're stuck with having me alone, eh?"

I said nothing. Richard turned over and slept off. I read another page before deciding to call it a night. I closed my book and laid it on my bedside cabinet, switched off the light, and then settled in for a comfortable sleep.

That night, I had the weirdest dream ever. I approached a door with my daughter, Linda, and my best friend's daughter, Gail, beside me. The three of us were dressed slutty and wore high heels. I knocked at a door, and seconds later, it opened to reveal Terrence, his friend, Ken, and Thaddeus Black; the three of them were naked.

"Are you boys ready?" I said. "Because we are."

The three of them smiled and invited us inside while the door shut behind us.

17

From a Gilf to a Snowbunny Pt. 2

I woke up on Saturday morning and went downstairs. Richard was in the kitchen eating breakfast cereal; Polly lay beside him on the floor, enjoying her meal. Richard was watching something on his phone and wasn't aware I'd entered the room until I came to the other side, grabbed a cup from beside the sink, and fixed myself some coffee.

"Morning," I said.

"Good morning. You look like you slept fine."

"I needed it," I ran my fingers through my hair as I sat across from him. "I'm going to see about going to the salon later. How's your day going to be?"

He switched off what he was watching on his phone before speaking. "I'll be going out to see my buddy, Avery. He's got this real-estate business offer he's been trying to talk me into, something about building condos. He figures I'll be a safe bet partnering with him."

"You don't fancy the idea?"

"I told him I was retired from all of that, but he keeps reminding me that I'm semi-retired, which means I can still slip into the pool and take a dip whenever I want."

"I think you should think about it. It'll be a great way to get you out of the house more often instead of being grumpy indoors."

"Who said I was grumpy?" He looked at me, but when I didn't reply, he gave up with a sigh. "Yeah, I guess I've gotten way too grumpy lately. This wasn't how being retired was supposed to feel. And with my ailment, I guess I can get up and do something besides playing golf."

"And besides chasing my lovers away," I quietly added.

That got his attention. His spoon dropped from his hand, and his look was sharper this time. The room stayed silent for a few seconds before he spoke.

"What are you getting at, Erica?"

"You know what the fuck I'm getting at, Richard. What? Did you think I wouldn't know what you did? Did you think I wouldn't figure it out or that you were so smart about what you did?"

"You're going to have to be specific about what you're talking about."

"I'm talking about Terrence," I said. "Remember him? The guy who used to be my lover, who you told me to invite over and have sex in front of you? The same man I haven't heard from since the past week?"

"I do know who you're talking about. The last time you mentioned Terrence, you said he'd left for Florida."

"He did, except I never would have thought you paid for him to leave if you hadn't shown me enough signals. Sure, I can't prove it—Terrence hasn't called me since—but I know you did something like that. You never forgave me for being with him behind your back, and you repaid me like this to get your sweet revenge."

"I know I got you to invite him over to have sex upstairs. Why would I go out of my way to do that then?"

"That's because you wanted to see for yourself how deep I was with him—that was a pity fuck for you, nothing more. But you did what you did, and since then, I haven't heard a word from Terrence. So far, you're not fucking denying it."

"I don't have to deny what I ain't done, Erica. If that's the word you want to hear from me, then let me be candid about it. I've got nothing to do about Terrence leaving for Florida. Is that what you want to hear, or have you got more accusations coming my way?"

"No, I don't. Terrence's gone, and I guess I'm moving on. It is what it is."

I looked into my cup of coffee and it felt lukewarm to consume. I emptied the coffee into the sink, rinsed the cup, and placed it in the dishwasher.

"Maybe I was still mad at what you'd done," Richard said as I left the kitchen. "Maybe I still nursed a grudge the way you let me discover what you were doing behind my back. Are you going to hate me now?"

I turned to look at him. "No, honey, I don't hate you. You did what you had to do, and that's all there is to it. But I would have loved it if you'd had the courtesy of letting me know."

"Letting you know what, Erica? Like you let me know you were cheating behind my back?"

"We've been over that part already, Richard," I replied. "You never seemed to have any problem before about me taking on a lover until lately. If you want to take your anger out on me for what I'd done, do it to my face."

"I don't have to do anything however you want me to, neither do I have to apologize for whatever I've done, Erica. Maybe in time, I'll forgive you properly for what you did. Until then, consider what I did as an act of kindness for my part."

"So you choose to be so magnanimous by making sure Terrence never called me again? That's your act of kindness? Well, you won, Richard. I'll give it to you, you fucking won."

I left the kitchen and carried on with the remaining task of cleaning up the house. Richard ignored me, and I was glad he did. I had nearly lost my nerve back then and was afraid of taking things further. I went upstairs to vacuum the bedroom with my nerves still throbbing with rage. I had been waiting since my last trip to Ken's place to let Richard have a piece of my mind. Though I lacked verifiable proof that he was responsible for Terrence leaving, every fiber in my gut told me he must have said something. I wasn't expecting him to admit it, but his initial silence when I confronted him had been enough. Richard might have won the battle, but the war was far from over. He was clueless about my dabbling with Thaddeus Black, and I wanted it to remain that way. He might have gotten rid of my esteemed lover, but he forgets there are still men out there who found me desirable. Why should I stoop to let him win?

I finished vacuuming the bedroom, then carted the hamper basket in the bathroom stacked with dirty clothes down to the washing machine in the basement. Richard did his line of cleaning; we were like quarrelsome siblings avoiding each other with little conversation. It wasn't the first time, and it certainly won't be the last.

Hours later, I showered and got ready to leave for the salon. Richard was in the living room talking to someone on the phone when I came downstairs and told him I was off. He grunted in response, and that was it.

I got into my car, started my car, and drove off. I made two phone calls along the way, ensuring my appointment would happen.

It was a twenty-plus minute drive to the hair salon, but I didn't intend to do my hair today. I had chosen the spot as a meeting place for Gail, so I called her after leaving the house to make sure she would be on time; my second call had gone to our impending date.

I pulled off the road into the short drive leading into the vast parking ground where the hair salon was located. I saw Gail's car and drove toward it. She sat behind the wheel smoking a cigarette. She looked up when I honked my horn and honked her in response as I drew alongside her.

"Hi," I said. "Are you ready to go for a drive?"

"I'm ready, Aunt."

"I'd like to give you another chance to say no. It's not too late to return home."

"Seems too late for me," she said.

"All right then. I'll lead the way while you follow behind."

As I drove for the exit ramp leading back onto the road, Gail started her car. I glanced at my rear-view mirror and watched Gail keep a reasonable distance behind me. If only

Sarah had any idea what I was about to do with her daughter. It made me recall last night's vivid dream I had. I wondered if there was any truth to that ever happening, or maybe it was nothing but my imagination.

My phone began to buzz; it was Thaddeus Black. I put the phone on speaker.

"Hi, Thad."

"Hi, Erica. Where are you heading?"

"Don't tell me you're following me," I checked my mirror, and though I saw Gail's Toyota less than a mile behind mine, I couldn't make out Thaddeus's in the traffic. "Where are you?"

"I've got my eyes on you, don't worry about finding me," he said. "Where are you heading?"

"Well, if you're so curious to find out, then you might as well keep following me, then you'll see."

"All right then, pretty lady. I'll follow."

He ended the call. I smiled and continued driving.

We arrived at Ken's apartment building. I pulled into the parking lot, and a minute later, Gail did likewise and parked beside me. I slammed my car door and went to join her. At the same time, Thaddeus Black entered the lot in his gorgeous Cadillac. I told Gail to give me a minute and approached his passenger side.

"Let me guess," I said as I leaned into his passenger window, "Richard called you up and told you to see where I'm going, right?"

Thad nodded. "He sounded angsty. He said you were heading to the hair salon—he gave me the address. This doesn't look like it."

"My hair appointment isn't until Monday. I'm here to see a friend."

"Let me guess, a male friend?"

"That's none of your business, Thad. But if you must know, yes."

"Who's the young woman with you?"

"She's interested in meeting my friend."

"You guys here to have a threesome? Any room for me?"

I laughed when he said that. "Is this off the record, or are you going to tell Richard what I'm up to?"

"Depends on you," he smiled back. "I scratch your back as you scratch mine, and everyone's a winner."

"Okay. Do me a favor and hang out here, and maybe I'll see about scratching your back."

"Promise?"

"Promise. I'll be back in a bit."

I returned to join Gail and led her toward the apartment building. She glanced over her shoulder toward the parking lot before turning to me.

"Aunt Erica, who was that?"

"A very dear friend," I replied. "Maybe after we're done here, I might introduce you to him. For now, come on, someone's already waiting for us."

We entered the building, and I led the way to the elevator to take us to Ken's apartment.

18

A Gilf and a Snowbunny Walked In

Inside the elevator, Gail tapped my elbow. "Remind me again, Aunt, who is he? I mean the man we're going up to see."

"I thought I'd mentioned that already?" I replied with slight irritation; Gail was eating at my nerves with her questions. "His name is Ken, and he's a good friend of mine who's going to show you everything you've been wanting to learn about this lifestyle of ours. That's all you need to know for now, and he knows we're coming."

"Sorry, Aunt. I guess I'm kind of nervous," she laughed. "I mean, this whole thing is starting to feel surreal for me."

"Don't worry, Gail, you're going to be fine. Trust me, I've been there before, so I know what you're going through."

She briefly fell silent, then: "Was my mom ever nervous with black men? I never could tell from the videos I watched of her."

I was saved by a *PING* noise, followed by the elevator doors easing open. We stepped into the corridor and I led the way to Ken's apartment.

"Don't worry about anything," I addressed Gail as we arrived at Ken's door. "Be your natural self and everything will be fine, you'll see."

I pressed his doorbell and waited. The door unlocked and opened to reveal Ken, looking suave and casual like he hadn't been expecting us.

"Nice to see you, Erica," he hugged and kissed my cheek, allowing us into his apartment.

"So nice to see you, Ken. I hope we didn't keep you waiting?"

"Not at all," he shut his door. "Was playing some video game to while away the time. Who's this lovely daughter of yours?"

I laughed when he said that; Gail laughed but blushed.

"This is Gail, my best friend's daughter." Gail shook Ken's hand. "Gail wants to learn some important sexual things, which is why I brought her over. I'd figured you'd be the perfect mentor for her."

"Oh, yeah? What sort of mentorship would she be interested in learning?"

This was how I wanted Ken to play things, which I had told him before arriving here. We sat down, and he went and brought us sodas; the cold sugar felt refreshing after the long drive. Ken sat with Gail on the sofa while I observed them. Gail couldn't stop blushing; she looked prettier and innocent—a rosy flower waiting to bloom.

"Maybe I should let my aunt tell it to you," said Gail.

"Oh, come on, Gail," I replied. "Let's not be shy. Go ahead and tell Ken what you have in mind. He won't bite."

Gail looked like she was about to choke on a nail. She was too shy to meet his gaze, and her cheeks glowed rosy red.

"My aunt here has a thing for dating black men," she said. "I wanted to know what's so attractive about black men that gets her going."

"Seriously?" Ken gave her a sly smile that charmed Gail; it let her know he knew exactly what she meant. "Well, you're so damn pretty. I'm going to need some history here. How long have you wanted to know about this?"

"It's been a while," Gail chuckled amid her blush. "I'm sorry, I'm acting all nervous."

"There's nothing to be nervous about. You're with good people here."

I checked my watch. We hadn't stayed up to ten minutes, but it was starting to feel like it. I then thought about Thaddeus waiting for me in the parking lot; he'd probably assume I was on my way. I excused myself and went to the balcony to gaze down into the parking lot. His Cadillac was there, reflecting the sun's light off its roof. I called him on the phone.

"Yo," he answered.

"Hi. I wanted to make sure you're still waiting."

"Are you on your way?" Thad asked. "It's getting lonely sitting here in my ride."

"I'll try to hurry things along; give me several minutes, okay."

"No problem. I'm still on the clock."

I ended the call, relaxed and reassured that he was waiting, and returned to the apartment.

I was stunned to see how fast things had gone when I left the room. Ken had drawn closer to Gail and was kissing her and caressing her chin while Gail adjusted her figure toward him, caressing the bulge under his jeans. I returned to my chair and sipped my soda while they continued to kiss like I wasn't there. Ken eventually pulled away, and Gail switched to seeming embarrassed when she saw my presence.

"Don't give me that look, Child," I addressed Gail. "I've been where you are plenty of times. Don't worry, you'll soon get used to things."

"Her class is about to begin," said Ken, who then spread his legs beside Gail. "Go ahead, babe, unzip me and get me hard."

"You sure?"

"You were touching me seconds ago, remember? You'd better continue what you started."

Gail glanced at me one second before applying herself to the task. She adjusted her frame and then leaned forward with both hands on Ken's crotch. She handled his jeans like a scientist working a dangerous chemical: unzipped his fly carefully, reached inside with her mouth hanging open while her eyes widened, and then uttered a throaty gasp when she encountered what she desired.

"Go ahead," said Ken, smiling with amusement. "Don't be shy, take it out."

"Oh my God," Gail murmured as she extracted Ken's cock out of its hiding place.

Gail's eyes expanded till they were the size of Dollar coins. I had to bite my lip to stop myself from laughing: the picture looked hilarious even though it was arousing. I felt like a true Gilf passing the torch to a snowbunny to carry on the tradition.

"Oh my God," Gail murmured repeatedly while gently stroking Ken's cock inches from her face. "It's so…it's unlike anything I've held or seen before."

Ken couldn't help but laugh, which compelled me to join him.

"Don't tell me your boyfriend hasn't something like this," he said.

"Fiancé," she corrected him. "And no, Jeffery doesn't have a cock as big as yours. Yours is way bigger…my God, I can barely wrap my fingers around it."

"You'd better get to sucking it then. This is the next big test."

Gail had a look of dread in her eyes as she inched toward his cock, breathing on it before letting it slip into her mouth. She gave his cock a smooching kiss, then slightly withdrew like she thought she had kissed a snake and expected it to bite her back. When that didn't happen, she drew closer and gave it a full plunge.

I continued to sip my drink while I watched. Gail was doing a credible job, although she didn't seem to be putting in much effort. She seemed to be sucking Ken's cock with reservation. I gave her a minute, and then my patience suddenly wore out.

"You're not sucking him hard enough, Gail," I said sharply, to which Gail looked at me like a student realizing she was failing at her lesson.

I sighed and got up, then approached them. "You don't suck a black cock as you would a white one. Get serious here, Gail—this isn't your fiancé's cock you're playing with. Watch me, let me show you how it's done."

I knelt before Ken just as Gail withdrew from his crotch. I grabbed Ken's cock almost like I wanted to rip it off his groin. I spat on his prick, and then opened my mouth and boldly swallowed him. Ken uttered a throaty gasp that indicated I was giving it to him properly. Gail looked with stunned eyes at my action. I bopped my head on Ken's crotch, sucking and slurping his cock like the whore that I was, never letting go an inch of his foreskin. My aggression and passion were in abject display in the way I choked on his prick.

I could feel myself getting moist underneath my jeans. I would have loved to keep sucking his cock, except I didn't want to keep Thaddeus waiting longer for me. Besides, this was Gail's workout to learn; I was merely doing what was necessary in showing her what being a black cock-whore was about.

I deep-throated him one final time before pulling away, gasping. I stroked his cock while wiping strings of saliva from my mouth, then turned to look at Gail with a fiery force she hadn't seen from me before.

"That's how you suck a black cock," I said, sweeping my hair from my face. "Put all your gut into it—every love and passion you can summon—don't ever back down. Got it?"

Gail nodded emphatically, still looking at me with a large pair of eyes. "I've got it, Aunt. I've got it."

"Good. Now have at it, and don't slip up."

I got up and let them continue from where they stopped. I returned to finish my soda and then grabbed my handbag.

"I'll call you in about an hour," I said. "Or maybe you can call me when you're done. I need to head downstairs and see someone."

I marched toward the door and let myself out of the apartment.

19

A Private Eye and
a Gilf in Heat

The elevator doors were about to close when I got there. I stopped the process and then jumped inside. The doors shut and the elevator drove to the ground floor. I pretended to imagine what was going on back in Ken's apartment. Gail was probably still blowing his cock, or he'd stopped to assist her out of her clothes before making her continue. Either way, her fun life is only getting started.

The elevator came to a stop and the doors slid open. Several people stood there waiting to use the elevator. I slipped past them into the lobby.

I was worried that in the space of leaving Ken's apartment, Thaddeus might have grown frustrated with waiting and blown off; I should have called before leaving to make sure. I came out of the building and began searching the parking lot. Thad's Cadillac was still parked where it was, and he saw me approach.

"Good thing you called then," he said as I approached his passenger window. "Are you done here? Where's your younger version?"

"She's upstairs getting busy with a friend. I've got about an hour before she finishes her lesson; you have any place where we can kill time?"

"Hop in first, and then we'll see."

I opened the door and slid into the passenger seat while he started his car. "As it turns out, my place is about ten minutes away; I'll see if I can make it in five."

"You take care of the driving," I slid my hand over his crotch. "In the meantime, I'll take care of this for you."

Thaddeus shifted his car into gear and pulled out of the building compound. I unzipped his fly and attended to his cock while he drove.

Thaddeus didn't make it to his house on Chamrose Avenue in five minutes; he did come close, though, in seven.

He pulled into his driveway and stopped ten feet from his house. I lifted my head from his groin and swept my hair from my face to see where we were. There were other houses similar to his, separated by a cobbled pathway leading to each front door.

"Which is yours?" I asked.

"The one on the left. Come on, I'll show you."

I sat upright and adjusted my blouse while Thaddeus tucked back his prick and zipped up his pants before opening his door. I came around his Cadillac and followed him to his front door. Thad unlocked it and allowed me inside before coming in and shutting the door.

His living room was moderately cozy. A large TV was mounted on the wall with an entertainment system beneath it; I inhaled an incense fragrance that reminded me of my bedroom. I looked around but saw no sign of any other inhabitant.

"You live alone?"

"If by alone, you mean have I got a woman around? The answer is no. But since you're here."

He drew me into his arms and our kiss immediately turned passionate. His hands grabbed at my butt while I slid my arms under his, making sure our bodies were together. Within minutes, he relieved me of my jeans and continued caressing my butt; he slid his hands under my panties to squeeze my flesh. It warmed me to him more; it reminded me of how Terrence used to caress me when we were together—*my God! I can't believe I've missed him so much.*

I had no idea where Thad wanted me—in his living room or elsewhere, preferably in his bedroom. We struggled and eventually stumbled on his sofa. My hand rummaged for his crotch. Thad unzipped his fly and whipped his turgid member out for me. I took charge and got to sucking him, kneeling on his sofa while he caressed my rump.

I don't recall how I got out of my clothes, but minutes later, so was him, and then he had me lying on my back with both legs spread apart. Thaddeus lowered himself over me, planting his knees on the sofa, and inserted his prick into my eager vagina. I yelped as he entered me. He eased his prick inch after inch, grunting as he buried his shaft inside my cunt. He grabbed hold of my feet, propping it against his shoulder while starting to jerk his hips. I grabbed him from behind and prodded him to continue. Like that, we began our jerky ride.

Gail was in her car waiting for me; I had called minutes ago to let her know I was on my way. The time was past the hour that I told her I would be returning. Sex with Thaddeus had been as smashing as it had been the last time we tousled. It was enjoyable fun knowing he was servicing me when he should be working for Richard, but it was my joy since Richard admitted to having a hand in getting rid of my boyfriend. Between first losing my boyfriend, finding out my daughter and her husband have a cuckold/cheating thing going on, and now having inspired my best friend's daughter into having sex with a black man weeks before her wedding, things sure were livening up for a horny Gilf like myself.

Life sure is sweet with exquisite irony when you have time to think about it.

I pulled into the parking lot and Gail left her car and came to my window. She wasn't looking shy or nervous compared to when we arrived.

"How did it go for you?" I asked.

"It was unexpectedly terrific," she exclaimed while laughing. "Far beyond anything I had in mind."

"I can almost smell him on you," I joked. "You're going to keep in touch with him, right?"

"Definitely," she said. "We exchanged numbers. But I'll still keep my mom from knowing."

"Your secret is still my secret, and vice versa. You'd better go get into your ride; let's leave this part of town."

"Sure," she stopped to look at me. "How about your friend?"

"He's gone to take care of other business," I said. "Come on, let's go get ourselves ice cream so you can tell me everything that went down. I know a great place."

Gail returned to her car while I reversed out of the lot. She waited until I was back on the road before trailing behind me.

Morning arrived.

I got up from bed, but Richard wasn't there. I felt like falling back to bed but decided what the hell; I swung my feet off the bed, found my slippers, did a few body stretches, and then left the room. I hadn't done yoga exercise in several days and my joints were starting to feel foreign to me.

The house was quiet like every other day, every other morning. Polly came to my attention as I came down the stairs. She licked my palm, then followed me into the kitchen, where Richard sat observing the rising sun outside the window. I kissed his cheek and exchanged morning greetings with him.

"You had anything to eat yet?"

"I was waiting on you," he said. "I also had something I wanted to get off my chest."

"Uh-huh," I murmured as I set about working the coffee machine. "Whatever you got on mind, dear?"

"I wanted to say that I'm sorry."

That stopped me. I looked at him, wanting to be sure he wasn't out of his mind. Richard had a contrite expression about himself. It had been a long time since I saw him in this low state of admission. Usually, Richard was too stubborn to ever admit to being in the wrong; this was one for the record books.

The coffee machine whirred into action. I offered Polly her dog treats, and when the machine clicked off, I filled two cups and offered one to Richard.

"What are you sorry about?"

"You were right about Terrence," he said. "Yes, I did talk to him about not wanting him to see you again. I've had time to think about it, and I'm admitting I was wrong for doing that."

"Did you threaten him?"

"I offered him some money, but he refused. But there was no threat."

I blew into my cup, letting the moment sink in, waiting for him to make any sudden reverse; a minute passed and nothing of such happened. This was so unexpected of Richard.

"What got you to do that?" I asked.

"A lot of things," he cleared his throat before continuing. "I was upset, though. I figured you wouldn't ever go behind my back to do something like being with another guy. It's been years since you and I had that sort of fun we used to have; it's depressing knowing I'm acting bitchy about this when I shouldn't."

"You were worried I'd leave you."

"That thought did cross my mind, sure. But now I figured I was stopping you from behind happy, which I shouldn't have. Like I said, I was upset you never told me."

"I'm sorry I didn't, too. I wanted to but knew you'd get upset and react the way you did."

"Yeah, I guess we're both sorry in that regard." He took a sip of his coffee, ruminating. "How come you didn't get your hair done yesterday?"

"I'll have it done on Monday; the saloon was packed."

"Oh. So, are you going to call Terrence?"

"Terrence is old news, darling. I've moved on, no thanks to you."

"I can give him a call if you want."

"The past is past, so don't bother. What I'd like is for you to allow me to have another lover. Is that all right with you?"

Richard shrugged. "Sure, I guess. Who you got in mind? Or maybe you can get Sarah to hook you up with one of her boy toys if she still has any around."

"I already have one, darling."

"That fast? Is he someone I know?"

I smiled. "Yes, darling, you do know him. He's coming by today."

Richard fixed me a sharp stare. "Who could it be then? Give me a name."

"Take a guess."

"I don't do guessing games, honey. Who is it?"

My smile widened at what I was about to say next. "I believe you know him. His name's Thaddeus Black."

The End